HIVE

Mickey Hadick

PARKSIDE BOOKS
HOLT, MICHIGAN

ISBN-13: 978-1-956533-02-6
Date of publication: October 3, 2021
Edition Revision: January 8, 2022

Cover graphics by 100Covers.com

Cover design by Mickey Hadick
Interior design by Mickey Hadick

Published by Parkside Books
Holt, Michigan
www.ParksideBooks.net

There is nothing called "partial freedom."

Nelson Mandela

Other books by Mickey Hadick:

Fiction:

Ten Stories
Sally and Billy in Babyland
The Forgettable Marriage of Lina and Joe
Welcome to Willieville
Ruthless

Nonfiction:

Boss Lessons

Sign up for updates and deals on books at:

MickeyHadick.com

HIVE

Mickey Hadick

CHAPTER ONE

Leah Davidson arrived at Decker's Cafe a few minutes early, hoping to talk with Abel, who had the
cursive writing lesson just before her own. Their
teacher, Jaylend, took a tea break between lessons, browsing the stacks of used books and old magazines along the
wall, allowing Leah and Abel more time to visit.

Leah would soon be sixteen years old and would have
to decide what to do with the rest of her life. For now,
with her studies complete and two baccalaureates earned,
she was enjoying what she thought of as days of freedom
spent talking with Abel while avoiding the future.

She knew it wasn't practical, but what she wanted
more than anything was to spend time with Abel here in
the cafe, drinking tea and coffee while reading books from
the collection. It seemed like they might explain all the
mysteries of the world, if only they spent enough time
there together.

They had known each other their entire lives, attend-
ing academic lessons together, church services, and now
cursive writing. She was well aware of her infatuation
with him—the heart flutters, nervousness, and obsession
over silly details—but also aware that things were not so
simple in this world as to spend time with whoever you

liked just because.

These moments were precious, but still she told herself not to stake too much meaning on them, as neither of them could control their own future. If they opted-in to the corporation's Terms of Service, they most certainly would not control their own future.

Abel stepped out of the cafe and for a moment they gazed at one another. "Leah," he said. "I wanted to talk to you."

Her heart fluttered. "What about?"

He seemed about to speak but motioned toward a table on the sidewalk.

The cafe was near enough to the raised train tracks separating Old Town from New Town to see the incorporated citizens waiting on the platform. With similar clothing, a helmet on their head and a visor over their face, it was impossible to tell one incorporated citizen from the next.

Below the tracks, street vendors from Old Town stood by their wooden carts, hoping to make a sale and earn a few creds. Dressed in vintage clothing, much of it repaired so often as to contain only a few threads from the original cloth, the unincorporated were as different from each other as the incorporated were alike.

As she sat down, Leah noticed Abel hadn't shaved that day. His beard and mustache were still just peach fuzz, but darker than his brown hair. Against his taupe skin, the peach fuzz looked good. It was appropriate for his age. And he'd inherited his mother's hazel eyes, which looked good. Or maybe that was just her infatuation talking.

"Did you have a good lesson?" she asked.

He nodded. "It may be my last."

"Why's that?"

"Of course I don't want to stop," he said. "I love

Jaylend. I love how she cares about writing, but also cares about us."

"She does," Leah said. "This is my favorite thing to do. I wish I could go more often, but my mother…is it your parents?"

Abel nodded. Again, he seemed about to speak, but then something caught his eye.

A robo-van descended fast and landed on the street, just missing a man carrying a bundle of goods in his arms. The man stumbled getting out of the way and fell, dropping his bundle. The man cursed at the robo-van, but a heavily armed security officer approached with his rifle trained on the man. Over the buzz of the rotors, Leah couldn't hear what the officer said, but the man ignored the barked orders and gathered what he could of his belongings.

"There you are," a woman called as the robo-van door opened. It was Abel's mother, Hannah Barker. She dragged Abel's seven-year-old sister, Ilasha, by the hand.

As the robo-van lifted off, a security van rolled along the street, stopping across from the cafe. Three more security officers stepped out of the van and took up positions, scattering Old Town opt-outs who watched.

"I worried you'd have taken the train before we arrived," Hannah said.

"What are you doing here?" Abel asked.

"I just need to speak with your teacher Janine," she said.

"Jaylend," Abel said, correcting her.

"Yes, I'm thinking of starting your sister, now that you're stopping. What do you think of that?"

Hannah didn't wait for her son to answer and smiled at Leah. "I haven't seen you in ages, my dear. How are you?"

"Fine, thanks," Leah said.

"I just love that you both spent so much time with cursive writing. I never learned it myself, but I'm convinced it makes you smarter, using more of your brain, and will pay many dividends once you start with the corporation. Good jobs are more competitive than ever. You don't want to end up in Fulfillment, right?"

Ilasha tugged at her mother's hand.

"Abel, be a dear and watch your sister," Hannah said. "I'm going to talk to your teacher. What was her name?"

"Jaylend," Leah offered.

"Yes, thank you," Hannah said. "Are you ready for the Opt-In Ceremony? I haven't even had a chance to talk to your mother about it."

"I'm not opting-in," Leah said.

"Oh? Well, I'm sure you'll be fine whenever you decide. Of course you know Abel is opting-in. Okay, well, excuse me."

She went inside the cafe and Leah waited a moment before looking at Abel, as he was situating his sister on his lap. The little girl was dark-complected like her brother. She had enormous eyes, jet black hair, and wore a designer dress with mid-calf socks and leather shoes. None of it had come from the R1 catalog. It was all custom and would have cost a lot of creds.

The girl stared at a pocket computer projecting a show with talking animals, the animals that used to live on the earth.

"I was going to tell you," Abel said.

"Okay," Leah said.

"Are you mad?"

"I'm not sure. We knew this would happen. I have to decide soon, too."

"My dad has been pressuring me. He wants me to get

started at R1. He's not a fan of young adults lazing about for years."

Leah looked at him, waiting for him to raise his face to see his eyes. "I know this is silly, but I thought we'd have this summer, you know, before we had to opt-in. We talked about going on a mission with the church, or we could keep going to the park, and keep taking lessons, and I don't know what else. But I just thought that."

Jaylend, her cursive writing teacher, had told them how it was before incorporation, when people young and old chose for themselves who would be their partner in life. Now, the corporation selected best matches for your happiness. Before incorporation, people often fell in love several times before settling down. Some, like herself, stayed single.

Jaylend had even shared books from before telling stories of love and heartbreak. The story of Romeo and Juliet was considered the ultimate love story. Leah thought it ridiculous, as the lovers were teenagers whose broken hearts would heal if only they hadn't felt trapped by their world. Their tragedy was more about how the young lovers' lives were determined at birth by their rank, and the stupid family feud that doomed them.

The only people now who avoided a planned and inescapable destiny were people like Jaylend, who had not opted-in, and lived under the old rules in the ruins of the city now known as Old Town. They had to arrange their own food, shelter and clothing, but the corporation could not tell them what to do.

"I'll talk to my parents," Abel said. "Maybe they'll let me wait."

Across the street, a security officer shoved the man with the bundle to the ground. He'd been too slow to leave, but now the bundle had come undone and his things—clothing and some food wrapped in a blanket—were scattered on the street.

"Your father is like a really big deal," Leah said. "He won't let you slack off just to hang out with me."

"I'll ask, though."

Leah stood up, worried about the man trying to gather his things as the security officer pressured him to leave.

"Leah?" Abel said.

"I'm going to help that man."

CHAPTER TWO

Abel felt like a fool as he watched Leah walk across the street. Of course he should have told her about opting-in before his mother blurted it out. He should have known his mother would blurt it out.

"Where is she going?" Ilasha asked.

"I think to help that man pick up his things."

Ilasha squirmed out of his lap, dropping the pocket computer. "I wanna' go."

Abel reached under the table to get the computer, and Ilasha slipped out of his grip. "Hey!"

He caught her, but then continued across the street to where Leah helped the man with his bundle.

Leah watched Abel approach and his heart fluttered. Her oval face was relaxed as she pulled her auburn hair back behind her ears. Her fair skin, much lighter than his own, was flush with a warm, rosy glow. The sun bore down on her face but she didn't squint, and her green eyes seemed ringed in gold. He was struck by the determination in her gaze, how it locked onto his own gaze and held him as she worked through the situation.

Two more security officers had arrived and gripped the man by the arm, pulling him away from Leah.

"What's the deal?" Leah shouted. "Leave him alone."

Two more officers ran down the street towards them, and Abel pulled Ilasha close with one hand, and reached for Leah's hand with the other. "I think we should go."

"I was just trying to help this man," Leah said.

The arriving officers inserted themselves between the man and Leah. "Please return to your home," one officer said, and pointed the rifle at the man's chest.

"They must be queen bees," the man said. "Slumming it in Old Town?"

Ilasha picked up a small wooden jewelry box, its deep luster reflecting her face.

"That's mine," the man said. "I'd like it back."

Abel took the box from Ilasha, who shouted in protest.

The officer shoved the man to the ground once more.

"There's no problem," Abel said. "Everything is fine."

The man's bundle was once again on the ground, but the security officer kept him from reaching it.

"Can I just get my stuff?" the man asked.

"He's frightening me," Ilasha shouted.

The two officers raised their rifles and shot the man, who fell backwards onto his own blood splatter on the street. As his legs twitched, the security officers opened fire on the half-dozen people watching from the sidewalk, killing them, and shot several more people in the back as they ran away.

Ilasha scooped up the wooden box from the pavement and Abel realized he had dropped it in the chaos.

As the man's left leg twitched, officers grabbed Leah and Ilasha and ran with them back toward the security van. Abel trailed after them, shouting for them to stop.

Security copters landed on the street. Abel could only watch as they loaded Leah into one of them. Then he was dragged into the other with his mother and sister, and the copter lifted off, the sudden ascent pushing them to the floor.

Ilasha still clutched the jewelry box, held just a few inches from Abel's face. His breath fogged over his reflection.

# # # #

The office in the center of their apartment had no windows and a single door. One wall was bare and white for computer projections. Shelves covering the other walls were packed with books from the pre-incorporation days.

Abel used the office as often as possible to read, journal, or just to sit. With the door closed, it was soundproof and blocked data signals. Not that Abel cared much about that.

His father, Gregory, left the door open unless his R1 business required privacy. With the door closed, nothing came in and nothing got out.

He closed the door now when he summoned the family inside to discuss the shooting. He and Hannah were on their second drink and sat on the sofa with Ilasha stretched out on their laps, asleep.

Abel sat at the desk, twirling his pen around his fingers.

"Tell me again," his father whispered, so as not to awaken Ilasha. "What happened?"

"Leah walked across the street to help a man pick up his things. They'd spilled when a security officer shoved him."

"Who was this man?" his father asked.

"Just some unincorporated old-towner."

"Do you know why the security officer shoved him?"

Abel shook his head. "Leah told them to leave the guy alone, and then I told them he wasn't doing anything."

"What were you thinking?" his mother asked. "I left you in charge of Ilasha."

"It was the girl," his father said. "The Davidson girl."

"Ilasha ran after her," Abel said. "I was chasing Ilasha."

"But I left her with you, not that girl."

"I said I was sorry."

"We don't want to wake Ilasha," his mother said. "This has been traumatic."

Abel sat back in the chair and threw up his hands. "Okay, fine. We wouldn't want to bother Ilasha."

"Have you taken any Steady?" his mother asked.

"No," Abel said. "I haven't taken any."

His father drained his glass and set it on the floor beside the sofa. "You know we worry about your welfare," he said. "You have to know how to behave to thrive in this world. It's difficult. That's why there aren't that many of us who can control ourselves and perform well enough."

"If you aren't careful, you'll end up in Fulfillment the rest of your life," his mother said.

"I guess I won't go to *Heaven* if that happens," Abel said.

"Do *not* make light of that," his father said. "You could end up in Family Valley. Any of us could. It happens more than you know."

"I know, Dad."

His father took the glass out of his wife's hand and drained it in a single gulp. "Why do you think the officers shot the man on the street?"

Abel walked around the desk and picked up the jewelry box that had fallen from Ilasha's grasp. "This was the man's. Ilasha picked it up after they had knocked him to the ground."

"That's ridiculous," his mother said. "You can't blame her for this."

"What did the man do?" his father asked.

Abel sat on the floor and leaned back against the desk, holding his head in his hands, his elbows propped on his knees. "He was just picking up his stuff."

"What did he say?"

Abel thought a moment. "The guy said something about queen bees."

His parents stared at him.

"What?" Abel asked.

His mother shifted Ilasha onto his father's lap and stood up, saying, "I need a fucking drink," as she left the room.

# # # #

His mother asked Abel to keep Ilasha company in the entertainment room and closed the office door.

Their apartment occupied half of the top floor of the building, with a covered patio outside, a spa, and the entertainment room besides their living space. The pool and spa had separate doors to the hallway and double doors to the interior space so that staff could maintain the mechanics without gaining entry to their apartment.

Abel tried to get Ilasha to sit outside on the patio, as he was not in the mood to be entertained. But she insisted in watching a show, and he was in even less of a mood to argue.

Their entertainment room was large enough to fit six more apartments. Abel had wandered the lower-level hallways one day, counting the doors, and concluding that the higher you were in the building, the larger your apartment.

The outfits worn by people on those lower-level floors were for the entry level office staff at the corporation. As their ranks rose at corporate, their floor and apartment size grew, along with the tailoring, cut and drape of the outfits available for purchase.

When he asked his father about this, the response was, "Of course that's how it works. What do you expect?"

They'd lived there, on the top floor, since Ilasha had been born. Before then, they had moved once or twice a year for as long as Abel could remember, each time into a larger place, but Abel hadn't connected it then to his father's promotions.

His father had been proudest of the last move. Knowing there were no more floors above them, Abel had been satisfied, too, thinking he could get used to a place.

Ilasha turned on the projector and selected a church-produced show for kids with music and dancing. She stared at first, still waking up from her nap. Then she nodded her head, rocked side to side, and soon she was dancing along with the kids in the show.

Abel watched the show, but he kept hearing the gunshots, and he pictured the kids in the show being shot by the security officers. He closed his eyes and rapped his fist against the side of his head, trying to chase away the images of blood and people falling face down in the street, their legs twitching, and the woman who cried out in pain until the security officer shot her in the head.

The door bell interrupted the show. Ilasha kept right on dancing, so Abel went to see who was at the door.

The panel next to the door displayed a fish-eyed view of several men waiting in the hall. The man in front was a tall white man with tan skin and a thin goatee. He was balding and wore the same type of suit Abel's father wore, meaning he was a big shot—but Abel had never seen him before.

Behind him was a tall, fit black man wearing a Security Officer's uniform for investigators and bureaucrats.

Behind them were four Security Officers in full combat uniform with weapons, armor, and helmets. Visors covered their faces.

Abel's stomach twisted and his heart pounded.

"Hello?" Abel asked.

"Merritt Rasmussen," the balding man in the suit said. "Here to see Gregory Barker."

"What is this regarding?"

"I want to make sure everyone is okay after the incident this afternoon."

Abel looked over at the still-closed door to the inner office. "Can you wait, please?"

"I just need to speak with your father and he hasn't answered my messages."

"Okay," Abel said. "Sorry."

Abel hurried to the inner office and pounded on the door. "Dad? They're here. They have guns." He knew they couldn't hear his words, but they would notice the pounding.

The door opened. "What?" his father asked.

Abel told him about the visitors, the guns, and did his best with the name the man had given.

"Where's Ilasha," his mother asked. Her eyes were red and swollen. She'd been crying.

"Entertainment room," Abel said, his voice shaking.

"You should take some Steady," she said and started down the hall.

"Hannah," his father called from the door. "I need you for this."

Returning, she handed Abel her drink. "Go check on Ilasha."

\# \# \# \#

Ilasha was bored, so Abel took her to her room and queued up a long story of animated characters she'd seen a dozen times already but wanted to watch again. Days when there was no school were often like this, with Ilasha bored and Abel pressed into finding some way to amuse her.

The shooting earlier in the day hadn't impacted her, and it was possible that being swept away, without having to look at the dead bodies, she saw it no differently than the animated stories she watched three or four times each day, characters on a screen who would appear again later, no matter what happened.

Abel was her age, eight, when she'd been born. When she was four, and in need of more distraction, they pressed him into service as her playmate around the apartment. Of course, they had staff around to help with other duties, but no other children her age with which to play until she started academic studies.

As she sat on her bed and stared at the computer, he used his pocket computer to monitor the front room. If his father didn't want him to observe, he would have turned off the feed with a snap of his fingers.

Abel's parents and the balding white man in the suit sat near the fireplace, each with a drink in hand. The black man stood near the entrance. The security guards must have stayed in the hall.

"I don't think there was any involvement by The Collective," Merritt, the balding man, said. "None of the deceased were on any of our known associates lists."

"Can you explain to me," Hannah said, "why the officers opened fire?"

"The A.I. identified a threat, and it showed the use of deadly force."

"And what was that threat?" Hannah asked. "I just want to know if it was against either of my children, or the other girl…"

"Leah," Gregory offered. "Davidson's daughter."

"Or was the threat something else?" Hannah added.

Merritt nodded. "I haven't seen the reports yet, but my team is reviewing the data, and I'll let you know."

"I was told that Security shot several bystanders," Hannah said. "Were they a threat?"

"The A.I. identified them as a potential threat," Merritt said. "It could have been imminent or in the future. If not, then just unfortunate collateral damage."

"Okay," Hannah said. "I'm glad the A.I. wasn't just eliminating witnesses."

"Darling," Gregory said. "We have to trust the A.I. Even if it makes mistakes, it learns."

"That's right," Merritt said. "But I believe that it was correct this time."

After taking a drink, Merritt said, "And how is Ilasha?"

"She's fine, thanks," Hannah said.

"Thank you for your time," Merritt said as he stood up. "I need to call on the Davidsons. Oh, and I brought Inspector Stetson Fox with me. He'd like to speak with your son, if you don't mind, to get his perspective on the events."

# # # #

Abel sat on the sofa between his parents and Inspector Fox sat across from them on a chair. The only adornments on his black uniform were a small Security Team insignia and a gold bar pinned to his collar showing his rank of inspector, first class. Now in person, Abel noticed his skin was sepia-toned, a dark reddish-brown, almost as light as his own, and the same shade as his father. Fox's features used to be called African heritage, whereas his own parents were Persian.

Fox had a pleasant face with widely set brown eyes and closely cropped dark hair. He seemed sincere and concerned about what had happened. The balding-man who just left—the big shot—seemed self-assured, and Abel had disliked him, showing no remorse for the violence of that morning.

Of course, it was possible the inspector was trying to seem concerned in order to get Abel to talk about what happened.

"Did you know Leah Davidson would be there at Decker's Cafe, in Old Town, this morning?" Fox asked.

"I guess I expected it," Abel said. "She always has the lesson after mine."

"And what lesson was that?" Fox asked.

"Cursive writing."

"Cursive writing?"

"Yes."

"Like with pen and paper?"

"Yes."

"Interesting," Fox said. "I hadn't realized anyone still did that."

"We feel it has benefits for cognitive development," his mother said.

Fox nodded. "Who is the teacher?"

"Kayla something," his mother said.

"Jaylend Foster," Abel said.

"This was vetted with Security," his father said. "We didn't just pick some Old Towner at random and entrust the safety of our children with her."

"There's been no kind of trouble at the cafe either," his mother said.

"I know," Fox said. "I haven't seen the background report on Ms. Foster, but I know that the cafe has a better variety of tea than I can acquire with my creds."

"Try their brownies," his mother said.

Fox smiled. "Noted. But, of course, things can change, so Mr. Rasmussen wanted me to double-check everything."

"Thank you," Abel's father said. "You'll let me know what you learn?"

"If there's anything unusual, someone will be in touch."

Abel scoffed. "Or the A.I. will tell a security officer to shoot us."

CHAPTER THREE

Abel carried Ilasha on his back to the roof-top roto-pad and into the robo-van their father ordered. He had motioned for them to remain quiet, and they lifted off into the late afternoon sky.

The passenger cabin had three padded benches and a small table in the middle. The A.I. piloting the craft kept the flight smooth enough to eat or drink without fear of spilling.

They lifted high over the city and moved toward the edge. Below them was the principal building of R1, which was wide and long, six stories tall, the tallest allowed in New Town.

At the other edge of the city center was the church arena, which also was six stories tall, but felt much bigger inside because they had excavated it ten stories down into the earth.

As they approached the edge of the city, he saw the outlines of roads, businesses, and houses consumed by encroaching vegetation.

Abel's father watched the skies carefully. When Abel followed his gaze, there were three roto-copters trailing after them.

His father motioned for Abel to remain quiet and revealed a gadget in his hand.

It was a small metal box that fit in his palm. It had switches and ports along two edges, and a button on the top. He set two of the switches and hit the button.

There was a low buzzing noise, and then he motioned for them to lean closer.

"We can talk," he said. "It masks our voices, ruins the data."

"Are you sure?" his mother asked.

"The copter is in privileged mode. No transmissions. But it still records everything on the flight data box." He pointed to his gadget. "This ruins it all, makes it look like a glitch."

"You better be right," she said, looking over her shoulder at the roto-copters creeping closer. "It looks like we're already in trouble."

"No. This is customary. They're just being careful."

"But we didn't do anything, did we?"

"No," his father said.

"At least nothing right now," his mother said. "Maybe the mistake was eight years ago."

"I don't understand."

"Is there any booze on this thing?" his mother asked. She opened a panel in the side and grabbed a bottle of wine.

"I need your full attention," his father said.

"Oh?"

"What's going on?" Abel asked.

His mother laughed. "It turns out," she said, "your sister is only your half-sister. She's not my daughter. I just carried her to term and birthed her, thank you very much."

"What?" He glanced at his sister. They'd put a visor on Ilasha's head before the flight and it engrossed her in whatever she was watching, oblivious to their discussion.

"I will explain," his father said. "Ilasha is the product of *in vitro* fertilization, from my sperm and an egg from Viktoria Olsen."

"Gross."

"Not gross," his mother said. "Just a cruel trick."

"Wait," Abel said. "The egg is from your boss, the CEO?"

"Yes, it's her egg."

"That's how he got this magnificent job," his mother said. "Here I thought he was a brilliant business executive and savvy negotiator. What a sucker I am."

"Hannah, please," he said.

Abel looked out the back window and the roto-copters were still following them. "I'm still confused."

"She's precious cargo," his mother said. "The Chief Executive Officer of R1, sovereign ruler of a third of the great country of Westhem, has entrusted the fruit of her loins to us to care for, protect and defend. If we endanger Ilasha, then we become the threat. That little girl is more valuable than the three of us combined."

"You don't have to be so dramatic," his father said.

"What is it they say around the office?" she asked. "Anyone can be replaced?"

# # # #

The robo-van returned to their rooftop. Before they entered the building, one of the roto-copters following them landed and two security officers in full gear and weapons, with visors covering their face, jumped out. A third officer stepped out, his face uncovered and without a weapon.

"Everything okay?" the officer asked.

"Yes," Abel's father said. "Just wanted to take a turn

around the city. It's beautiful at this time of day."

"We needed to unwind," his mother added.

"Have a good night," the officer said.

Outside their apartment, the house staff waited with the evening meal. Abel took charge of Ilasha as his mother supervised the staff setting the dining room table. His father sequestered himself in his office.

His mother dismissed the staff for the evening after they served the food and instructed the morning staff to arrive early to deal with the mess.

They ate in relative silence, with Ilasha's pocket computer providing a constant drone of noise as she watched another show, taking advantage of their parents' distraction.

"Is everything alright?" his mother asked as his father made yet another trip to the office.

"Catching up on things," he said. "I've been derelict all day."

His mother went into the office, then came out, then returned. They both came out a few minutes later and declared the meal at an end.

"Keep an eye on Ilasha?" she asked. They returned to the office and closed the door.

"What's going on?" Ilasha asked.

"They're talking about something," Abel said.

"About what?"

"Nothing you or I need to worry about."

"Do I have to go to school tomorrow?"

"Yes."

"Good," Ilasha said. "Today was boring."

Abel supervised Ilasha's bedtime preparations. When she was asleep, he stayed within earshot of the office and heard the door open and close a few more times.

He contacted Leah with his computer later that

evening. "You okay?" he asked.

"I guess," she said. "That was sickening."

"Are you going to take Steady to help you sleep?"

"No," she said. "I still hate the idea of that stuff. I'm going to practice my breathing exercise until I pass out."

"Me too."

"How's Ilasha?"

"Oblivious. I'm not sure she registered what was happening."

"Ugh. I wish."

He wanted to talk to her about baby dragons and queen bees but, after this morning, he knew it was one of the most sensitive things he could bring up. Even though neither one had opted-in, and they were using a secure channel, there was no guarantee the A.I. wasn't listening to the call.

"I'm going to postpone my opt-in."

"What did your parents say when you asked them?"

"I haven't asked them yet."

"Oh."

"I'm just going to tell them I'm not doing it. If they make me, I'll just not say the words or sign the paper."

"Don't do it just because of me."

"That's part of it," Abel said.

"Good luck."

Hoping to extend the conversation, Abel said, "Did the inspector visit?"

"Yeah," Leah said. "My dad doesn't want me to talk about it."

"Mine either."

"Shoot," she said. "I have to go."

"You think you'll go back to Jaylend for your next lesson?"

"I don't know," she said. "I'll call you before."

CHAPTER FOUR

Leah tried to calm down after the incident in Old Town, but when she lay on the bed and closed her eyes, she heard the gunshots and had to remind herself it was over. Unable to sleep, she paced the room or tried to distract herself with something on her computer, but the image of the dead sprawled on the street was all that she saw.

She'd never wondered about the armed security officers patrolling the sidewalks, or the vans rolling along the street, or the roto-copters overhead.

Until that moment, she'd been excited about things in her life. Completing her academics with honors filled her with pride. She loved her family, and the things they got to do because her dad had a good job at R1. And there was her friend, Abel, whom she liked a lot.

She loved cursive writing and Jaylend's stories about life before incorporation. It seemed like an adventure story, how the world went through disaster after disaster, but somehow people survived. Then R1 took over managing the cities and states, and then pretty much everything else, and things got better.

She learned in school about how R1 saved the world, rebuilt the cities, and figured out how to feed everyone and give them jobs.

She learned from Jaylend that there had been terrible fighting for years before they settled things. Jaylend said little more than that, and so Leah assumed it was because things were better now.

Seeing people gunned down in the street, she realized that the fighting meant people died. People were shot where they stood, or shot as they ran away. Those people lay in a pool of their own blood, groaning, until they died.

Leah's mother opened the bedroom door. "Sweetie? How are you?"

Leah shook her head.

"Your father says he talked to you about what happened. Do you need some Steady?"

"I don't want to take Steady."

"You look terrible. Have you slept?"

"No."

"Well then, that's your own fault," her mother said.

"I didn't do anything."

"It's been a day all ready," her mother said. "Go for a walk in the park."

Leah turned away from her mother and faced the wall.

"I'm going out," her mother said. "I guess you'll do whatever you want."

In the evening, her father knocked on her door. "Leah, we're going to eat now."

"I'm not hungry," she said. She was hungry, though. She hated the fact that her body wanted food when the world, it seemed, was not what she thought it was.

"I think it's important you eat," her father said. "Will you join us for a little while?"

Leah lingered on her bed for a minute before getting up. Her computer, triggered by the movement, switched to mirror mode and projected her self-image. Her auburn hair needed to be brushed but it fell on her shoulders well-enough for a family dinner. A half dozen pimples were scattered across her face, and would remain there until they went away naturally, as Leah refused to submit to the clear-skin treatment her mother suggested. She liked her natural eye-color, green, and wondered what Abel thought, as the color matched his sister's.

The dinner table looked a mess with food platters and silverware scattered about. Her mother had dismissed the serving staff and pressed Karas, their firstborn, into service instead.

"Why isn't she doing anything?" Karas grumbled.

Her mother glared. "I promise she'll set the table when you're nearly murdered by The Collective."

"It wasn't The Collective," Leah said. "They were innocent people."

"Let's keep our voices down," her father said.

At last they were seated and Leah's father smiled. This comforted Leah because without a smile he looked like every other middle-aged white man in New Town: short hair and dressed in a suit by R1. Of course, people wearing visors looked like each other, but she hardly saw them as people. They were more like robots.

When her father smiled, she saw all the jokes he made around the house, the things he did to make their family happy, and how proud he was of his daughters.

"Your mother ordered your favorite," he said, and passed along a platter of noodles.

"I did?" Tyra asked. She had a long nose and wide-set,

blue eyes. Her hair was straight, off the shoulders and dyed dark brown, which made her skin seem paler than it already was.

Karas raised her head. She'd been watching something on her computer resting on her lap. Karas took after their mother with blue eyes and a long nose, but with hair dyed yellow and frequent tanning, you had to look long enough to see the similarity. "Well, if it isn't Mopey Dick," Karas said.

Leah frowned. "When did you read Moby Dick?"

"What's Moby Dick?" Karas asked.

"It's a superb book about an obsessed sea captain hunting a whale."

"Is that why they went extinct?"

"No," Leah said. "You didn't know about the book when you referred to me as Mopey Dick?"

"I just meant you've been moping around all day."

"Of for fuck's sake," Leah said.

"Language," her mother said. "I don't want to hear vulgarities."

"I witnessed the murder of nine innocent people yesterday," Leah said. "Nothing is more vulgar than that."

"It's twelve," Karas said, holding up her computer. "There was more shooting after they flew you out of there."

"Okay, thanks for that," Leah said. She got up from her chair.

"Leah," her father said. "Please stay with us."

"They're saying it was a terrorist attack by The Collective," Karas said. "You're kind of famous, except that you're not in the videos and they don't mention your name. But I told Ashton, and he said everybody is already talking about it."

Leah burst into tears and ran to her room.

Her father came in and sat on the bed. "Sweetie," he said. "I want you to know that you're safe. I can promise you nothing like that will ever happen to you."

Leah wiped her nose and sat up. "I'm terrified that it happened because of me," she said. "That because I'm your daughter, and you're an executive with R1. Those fucking monster security officers shot those innocent people."

"I know, sweetie."

"That man was just trying to live his life, and first they knocked him down, then chased him away, and then they shot him."

"It made no sense," her father said. "Is there anything I can do for you now? We can get someone to talk to you. This is a lot to figure out."

"All I want," Leah said, "is for everybody to live their life the way they want to without fear of being shot dead in the street."

"I want that too, sweetie," he said.

"But I don't know how to make that happen."

Her father nodded. "I'm afraid the world is more complicated than just you or I can understand."

"So that means there isn't anything we can do?"

"Not right now."

"Can we at least try?" she asked.

"I promise you," he said. "If there's something I can do, I'll try."

# # # #

Leah was almost certain she didn't want to be at the church arena for the Opt-In ceremony. She was angry at Abel for not taking her calls this past week, and also for not explaining why he hadn't postponed his opt-in when he said that he would.

She had been unable to escape the ceremony. Her father, as an R1 vice president, would be on the stage as a dignitary, and her mother was on the reception-organizing committee. Karas was in charge of the punch bowl. With video-drones hovering over the crowd, streaming their faces on the big screen, she couldn't even hide.

Watching Abel sign the agreement and change his life forever, without so much as a quick chat on the decision, turned her stomach.

But he was still her friend, and she'd never forgive herself if she didn't witness this most momentous decision.

Still, it would have been nice if he'd taken her call, or somehow sent her a note.

Her parents gave her the option of staying in their suite on the condition she sat in the seats overlooking the arena. It was easy enough to ignore the smattering of people in the neighboring suites, but she dreaded the possibility of a video-drone find her up there, alone, and projecting her face for all to see.

The church arena had seating for over forty-thousand people, and they held services every day, and twice on Saturday. There were, of course, smaller church venues throughout the city and the church village. The city had over a million opt-in residents, all of whom had to attend church at least once a week, and some churches accommodated just a dozen people at a time, but the services ran on loop, and you only needed to stay there a minute to get credit.

It all seemed ridiculous to Leah. There were hundreds of thousands of people in Old Town, and they didn't attend these churches. Of course, her mother pointed out that none of them would ever go to Heaven. When Leah pointed out that they seemed happier than everybody in New Town, they sent her to her room with no data.

"Never say such a thing again," her mother said. "Don't even think it, or none of us will go to Heaven."

She could try to call Abel now, before the ceremony began, but it seemed even less likely he'd take the call now after ignoring her all week.

On the altar, her father sat in the rank and file of R1 executives. In the front row, she could pick out Abel's father, seated to the right of Viktoria Olsen, the Chief Executive Officer.

Her mother and sister, along with Abel's mother and sister and a few hundred others, sat in an exclusive section on a raised platform assembled on the arena floor. Between them and the altar were the opt-in candidates, each dressed in a uniform of powder blue, in rank-and-file seating of their own.

The ceremony began with music and introductions. Disgusted with herself for not trying harder to talk to Abel before this moment, she ran back into the suite and out into the hallway.

The candidates would line up and process across the altar, signing the opt-in agreement and shaking hands before returning to their seats. She could make her way to the edge and at least let him know she was there, maybe shout to him. If she was lucky, she could hold his hand for a second as he walked by.

She took the elevator to the arena floor and had to wait to pass through security. By the time she was free to walk, she was second-guessing herself.

He hadn't tried very hard, as far as she knew, to contact her. Why should she go out of her way?

Then again, maybe he had tried, and she would learn what was the matter by seeing his face.

Either way, it was fine because they were just friends. Nothing more.

Her progress was slow because the crowd was heavy. People were piling into the arena seating. Leah's frustration grew to anger, as none of these people would care about the ceremony. Not only did this count as a church service, but the opt-in ceremony meals, provided free to all in attendance, were legendary.

The keynote speech by Viktoria Olson began:

"Citizens of Westhem, good day to you."

The crowd responded in unison, "And also to you."

"I am proud and honored," Viktoria said, "to lead this organization that provides for the livelihoods, food, shelter and medical care of millions of people in the western division of R1. We're not just running a business… we're caring for each other.

"And remember, we are one under the sun."

She asked everyone there to repeat it with her, and it became a chant, "We are one under the sun. We are one under the sun. We are one under the sun."

When they quieted down, she resumed her speech. "As this beautiful place of worship continues to fill up, I am thrilled for the future this promises to all of us and the world. We have all suffered from the catastrophic problems the world has endured.

"But together, we will continue to heal the world. Together, we will make Westhem great. Together, we all go to Heaven."

The crowd erupted into thunderous applause. Leah had only gotten as far as the walking ramp to the floor level, but now she could finally make progress.

Again she wondered if she was just being silly.

As she stepped onto the arena floor, the Chief Minister was at the lectern and spoke: "Citizens of God, good day to you."

Once again, the crowd responded, "And also to you."

"It does a soul good to see so many people ready to opt-in, to dedicate their lives to the work of the people, to care and provide for each other."

Leah stepped past those seated on the side—family members, most likely, but not of any status that would have gotten them into the exclusive section with a better view of the altar.

"Not that long ago," Chief Minister Rohn said, "the world was a dark and terrible place. Those of you old enough to remember, you know that thoughts of end days crossed your mind. I know you wondered if God had forsaken us, leaving us to starve, and suffer, our hearts filled with hatred for one another.

"I know this to be true because those thoughts crossed my mind, and hatred filled my heart.

"But I'm glad I did not abandon God altogether, for he hadn't abandoned us. We wouldn't be here, with such abundance as this, if he didn't love us..."

Leah came to a barrier separating the crowd from the opt-in candidates. She looked and found Abel, two rows closer to the altar, and moved along the barrier so that he might see her as well.

"Abel," she said.

"Leah!" he rose from his seat and stepped past the other candidates until only the barrier separated them.

"Hey," she said, at a loss for words.

"You came."

"Yes. Congratulations."

Abel nodded. "I'm sorry I didn't call you. My parents have been weird, and they made me promise to opt-in. I've never seen them like this."

"It's fine. I have no right to ask you to do anything."

"They promised me I don't have to get a job or anything, for as long as I want. We can see each other every day, if you want."

Leah liked that he wanted that, but she also knew that once you opt-in, things are different. You can't do just anything you want to do, so...

She realized there was no more speech being delivered. She glanced at the altar, and the Chief Minister was looking back. He smiled.

There was no sound, in fact, in the entire arena. Abel glanced over his shoulder, and the other candidates were smiling at them.

Above the altar, on the eighty-foot screen, Leah and Abel were projected in profile. A camera had zoomed in on them.

"It's okay," the minister said. "We'll wait."

The crowd erupted in laughter, then roared with cheering and applause.

Mortified, Leah said, "I'll talk to you at the reception."

Abel made his way back to his seat. Leah, hoping to slink away, instead was escorted back to the suite by a team of Church Safety Stewards.

CHAPTER FIVE

Inspector Stetson Fox watched the opt-in ceremony from the first row of the upper level seats, which provided an unimpeded view of the exclusive seating section, the opt-in candidates, and the altar. He was there to investigate the incident involving the children of two R1 executives.

One child was rumored to have hatched from an egg provided by the R1 chief executive.

Some might see this investigation as an opportunity to impress important people and to make a name for oneself. Stetson did not see it like that.

He hoped this high-profile investigation led to nothing, allowing him to go back to his ordinary duties and the semblance of a normal life.

He did not like this world or the people who were in charge, but he liked the opportunity to investigate wrongdoing, as he did in the days before incorporation. He investigated what they then knew as white-collar crimes: financial fraud, insider trading, and tax evasion.

Back then, the hard part of the job was to identify the laws being broken. After centuries of interpretation, you had to know the case history of the very complicated laws, rules and policies of local, state and federal governments.

Something that seemed wrong could, in fact, be legal. Or that thing could be so difficult to prove in court that no one was prosecuted.

You had to account better than the bad guys' accountant, and lawyer better than the bad guys' lawyer, and grift better than the grifter behind the con. That was then.

Now it was as simple as describing the events and circumstances to the A.I., grab coffee while it thought about it, and then read the machine's decision.

If a party, as the agreements described a person, violated any of the terms of service as described by their signed opt-in agreement, they were subject to disciplinary action of the corporation.

What happened after that, Stetson didn't know. He knew enough not to ask, either.

He scanned the crowd through binoculars. The binoculars were ancient technology, and he was the only guy on the security team still using them. The modern tool was a high resolution camera with great optics. They attached to your pocket computer, and could even target and track individuals.

Stetson preferred the older technology, allowing him more discretion on what he told the A.I. With the digital cameras and computers involved, everything was data and only the machine decided what the data meant. There was no room left for interpretation.

Everything here today seemed simple enough, though. The parents were in the stands. Abel was in his uniform and waiting while the big-shots talked on the altar. The only person missing was Leah, and he knew for a fact that she had entered the building.

Then Abel and Leah appeared on the projection screen above the altar. That was not usual. Something was unresolved between them.

They both skipped their cursive writing lesson the previous week which he assumed it was the parents intervening because of the incident the week before. Now he had something to think about.

The ceremony was without further incident. He confirmed through his binoculars that Leah watched from the arena seating of her family's suite. Unlike almost every other person in attendance, she didn't look at her pocket computer at all. Leah sat watching from above, shifting in her seat, and leaning forward when Abel crossed the stage.

Meanwhile, the Church Safety Stewards, stationed in each section and every intersection, seemed relaxed, showing nothing else had transpired. Their event security was better than the corporation's. The church security established multiple inspections and checkpoints at all services. Even at the tiniest church locations, security greeted you upon entry, and security watched during the service, like so many angels watching you in heaven.

After the ceremony, the crowd moved and flowed in currents, some toward the exits, others toward the arena floor, and those on the arena floor were chased away by the event staff removing chairs so that the reception buffet could be set up in their place. It reminded Stetson of a nature film he'd seen in his youth of two colonies of migrating ants as their paths cross and a pitched battle ensued.

Here in the arena there was no fighting—people who had survived this long had learned how quickly justice was meted out for rule breakers—but there would be plenty of jostling for position to get a portion of the food.

By the time he'd gotten to the arena floor, they served the reception food. The crowd had thinned out considerably because the church understood that putting food and drink outside, along the exit paths, was the quickest way to turn over the seats so another crowd could enter.

Stetson moved in close to the two families on the floor. The Davidsons, missing Leah, were waiting to congratulate the Barkers, who stood together surrounded by a throng. Greg, the father, was the highest ranking R1 executive with an opt-in.

Stetson's boss's boss, the Chief Security Officer, chatted with the elder Barker before moving on. Barker, recognizing Stetson, must have said something, because Stetson's boss's boss pulled him aside.

"You're on an official investigation?" Rasmussen asked him.

"Yes sir," Stetson said.

"I thought the A.I. green-flagged it."

"Just completing my work, sir. I like to be thorough."

"Do your job, but don't be a nuisance."

When Stetson resumed his surveillance, the Barkers were gone and the Davidsons, still missing Leah, were all busy on their pocket computers.

It was probably nothing, but he would get close to Leah and Abel if they were still in the building, observe their behavior first hand and then leave the rest of it up to the A.I.

CHAPTER SIX

Leah waited outside the Barker's suite. She could have fought her way through the crowd and down onto the floor, but they would have to return here.

Besides, now that it was over, maybe he could take a minute to call her.

She used her pocket computer to watch the live video feed of the arena floor. People mingled and shifted around and waited in line for food. She thought she saw her parents and Abel and his family at one point, but she wasn't sure.

They arrived at last: Abel's father and mother hurrying, and Abel and Ilasha, holding hands as they trailed behind.

The parents slowed their approach. "I'm sorry, but..." Abel's father said.

"It's the Davidson girl," his mother said. "Lina?"

"Leah," Abel said. "She's my friend."

"Okay," Abel's father said. "But we have to go. There's no time."

"It'll be fine," his mother said. She took Ilasha by the hand and hurried inside the suite.

"Congratulations," Leah said. "I assume you're thrilled?"

"I'm not," Abel said. He studied her, seemed about to say something else, only sighed.

"What is it?" she asked. "I'm your friend. You can tell me."

"The thing is, I can't. I had to promise."

"Who did you promise?"

"My parents," Abel said. "They made me. They also didn't want me talking to you."

"What did I do?" Leah asked.

"Nothing."

"Do they not like me?"

"It's not that."

Leah tried to look at his eyes, but he stared at the floor. "Do they want you to marry someone, now that you've opted-in?"

Abel groaned. "I can't say it."

He motioned with his hands at the walls, and Leah understood that the microphones in the church, like those the corporation installed all over the city, recorded everything said.

"Remember what Jaylend taught us?" Leah asked.

Abel stared, not understanding.

She held her hand out before him and brushed the palm with her finger. The light of understanding clicked in his eyes.

They stood side by side, their arms intertwined. Abel held her right hand in his left and used his right index finger to make the shorthand notations they learned from Jaylend along with cursive writing.

When he was through, and she worked out what he'd written on her palm, she gasped. He had written: "We are leaving the city."

She took his hand in hers and wrote, "Where?"

"A dragon's lair," he wrote back.

Leah didn't know what to say. They were just legends, she thought. Things that kids talked about like fairy tales. No one ever went to a dragon's lair.

"When?" she wrote in his hand.

"Now," he wrote.

"For how long?"

"I don't know. I'm sure I can see you soon, though."

With nothing more to say, their fingers intertwined, and he wrapped his arm around her.

She might have told him how much she would miss him, but he was sobbing, and she was certain he felt the same way.

The suite door opened and Abel's mother paused a moment. "Abel," she said. "You need to change your clothes. Now, okay?"

They clung to each other for another moment, then Abel pulled away.

"See you later," he said.

Leah nodded. She said nothing because she worried she would cry and not be able to stop if she spoke at that moment.

After the door closed, she lingered, thinking he might open the door again, but a figure emerged from around the corner of the hallway.

It was Inspector Fox, who had talked to her after the incident at the cafe.

"Good day to you," he said.

Leah cleared her throat. "And also to you."

"You seem upset," Fox said. "May I ask why?"

Leah shook her head. "I'm fine."

"That was Abel Barker you were talking with?"

"I need to go," Leah said.

"If I could just ask you one more thing—"

Leah didn't wait. She hurried to her family suite, crying as she ran through the hall.

# # # #

Abel lay awake listening for sounds in the hallway. They had given him his own room at the church retreat center, where he'd gone with his family after the opt-in ceremony. His parents and sister slept in the next room.

He opened the door and walked down the hallway to the common area. At one end was a large fire pit, which was dark and dormant. Near the main door was a reception desk where a clerk sat staring at a computer projection.

There was an activity center near the reception desk. In earlier retreats, Abel had used the computers there for games with friends. There was a church specific messaging app, and he might be able to use that now to get a message to Leah.

He hated how they parted. He worried that he'd said too much, and that one word uttered by Leah could get them in trouble. He also worried about not seeing her and wanted to stay in contact.

The clerk, a young man in a church uniform, didn't so much as glance at Abel as he walked past the desk.

Abel found the room, flipped on the light, and sat down at a desk. He entered his username, password and pin—as he had done dozens of times before on the church network—but it denied him access.

He tried again, and again, and again.

Frustrated, he left the room to go talk to the clerk at the desk.

As he entered the common area, there were two

church Safety Stewards at the desk. Abel walked back toward the residence area and the Safety Stewards followed.

"Excuse me," one of them said.

Abel waited for them.

"Your father forbade your use of computers," the steward said. "Were you aware?"

Abel shrugged.

"We're instructed to take you to him. Will you come along then?"

"I guess."

They walked, one in front, the other behind, to the end of the residence hall. One steward knocked on the door.

"Can I just go to my room?" Abel asked.

The steward shook his head.

Abel's father answered the door, listened to the explanation, and thanked the stewards. Then he took Abel to his room.

"I'm just bored," Abel explained. "And this is so weird."

His father leaned against the closed door. "Was it about that girl?"

Abel felt the blood rush to his cheeks. "I just want to talk to her. I was rude."

"You can't," his father said, his voice just a whisper. "I'm sorry but you can't."

"When can I?"

"I'm afraid you just won't be able to. Ever."

"But when are we coming back?"

"We're not," his father said. "Your mother and I have decided it's best for the family that we break free of R1."

"That's impossible."

"I'm sorry, son, but in time, you'll understand."

His father opened the door to leave. Abel ran at him,

pushing his way through the doorway.

The Security Stewards waited in the hall and grabbed him, lifting him off his feet as he struggled.

Abel shouted and screamed, but they carried him back into the room and held his arms until he stopped kicking.

"We're leaving in the morning," his father said. "You'll understand later."

"I won't go," Abel shouted. "I just won't go."

The stewards sat him on the bed. "Stay here," one steward said. "That way you won't get hurt."

"Go to hell," Abel said.

They released their grip, and Abel considered trying to run again, but there would be another chance. There had to be. He'd find a way to just not go, even if he had to walk back to New Town alone.

"Okay," his father said.

"What was the point of opting-in?" Abel asked. "What was the point of anything?"

"We'll talk more tomorrow, and I'm confident you'll understand."

CHAPTER SEVEN

Stetson went to the office, rather than go home. He didn't know what he knew and wasn't sure what he learned at the church arena, but he felt an ancient urge to figure it out.

One of the younger inspectors would have logged into their Security Investigation System, accessed the Investigation Wizard, and entered what they knew about the case as the system prompted them. When that was complete, they would have ended their investigation and could forget about it.

In a day, or a year, or maybe longer, if the A.I. decided there were violations of the terms of service, it would issue an order and a different team would notify the parties and gather them. The investigator might never know what happened to them.

Stetson was still avoiding the computer system on this case and only had his pocket notebook with him, and a pen he respected but didn't love. On an empty page, he wrote their names, job titles, and roles of the people related to the case. He wrote how they related to each other, if at all. He wrote where they had been, and where such people could go in this world.

Stetson wrote what he was told had happened and

who told him. He wrote what he had seen with his own eyes.

All these things he could have done from the relative comfort of his one-bedroom apartment. But what he did next, he didn't want to do from his apartment.

He logged into their Security Investigation System and brought up the permanent records of all the involved parties. The system displayed the records whether or not they had opted-in, but it wasn't a lot of information. The permanent records were listings of life events, kind of like a resume, with the added touch of any possible or actual terms of service violations.

Only the A.I. knew the details of the events or violations.

These limits, Stetson understood, were because of the terms of service. The corporation had the right to collect a staggering amount of data about individuals, but it limited the use of that data.

The exception was that the A.I. could correlate the data, make connections, and infer violations. And everyone in this world who opted-in had granted that A.I. full control and authority over the data.

Stetson, when it was his time to opt-in, saw the clause that would doom them all to this data-driven autocracy. They buried it in the middle of a thick paragraph about rights and protections. If anyone had bothered to read the terms of service, they most likely would have been numb to the language used by the time they fought their way through that paragraph.

It read, "The corporation's system is hereby granted access to process and maintain the aforementioned data, and it may compile summary reports on various topics to employees of the corporation, but it will at no time divulge the data about any single person to an employee of the corporation, nor any person under the corporation's jurisdiction, nor any third parties outside of its jurisdiction."

Even for those who understood the clause, as Stetson did, they had no choice. He had no one left in the unincorporated world to care for, so it seemed like it wouldn't matter to him. Now it felt like his single greatest failure of cowardice.

The dirty trick the corporation played was the summary. If the summary report declared that an individual had violated the terms, then that was all that they needed to do anything to that person. All their privileges were revoked, and they had no right to anything. That person could be banished to Family Valley, assigned to a penal colony, or their organs could be harvested.

No data about the person was ever divulged. Only the A.I. knew what happened, and its decision sealed the person's fate.

Stetson ran a few queries about recent corporate events, activities, and changes in structure. He browsed through a listing of known associates of The Collective. He looked through the statements issued by the corporation about new business opportunities, supplies being delivered, and product shipments to the other corporate divisions.

None of it seemed out of the ordinary, but he kept digging, building the case the old-fashioned way.

On Monday morning, his boss, Priti Leaf, the Chief Inspector, found Stetson at a desk, scrolling through corporate statements.

"I thought we agreed we would wrap the investigation on Friday," she said. "The boy opted-in, yes?" Priti was a tall woman with dark hair and a dark complexion. Stetson had always admired her ability to betray little of her thinking with her expression, but that the tone of her voice would show the edge of anger when warranted. She had deep-set eyes that were perpetually in shade, adding a sense of foreboding to each encounter.

"I had a few loose ends," Stetson said. "I need to talk to one more person."

"Put what you have in the A.I. and let me know. We have other investigations."

"This one is different."

"You have something?"

"I have a theory."

Priti laughed. "Okay, well, I know you had experience before incorporation, but you need to do it the corporate way now."

"It sometimes misses things," Stetson said.

"No one ever got sent to Family Valley for using the A.I."

"I just worry about people who get sent to Family Valley for no good reason."

Priti tapped the top of the computer on his desk. "Talk like that gets people sent to Family Valley."

"I'd like to speak to the Chief."

Priti, who had started away, turned and stared. "I'm the only chief you need to worry about."

"He requested me, and he asked that I provide updates. I'd like to speak with him now."

"I want you to tell me what you have, first."

Stetson wasn't one hundred percent certain, but he had enough data to trust his inclination. "If the Chief Security Officer tells me, himself, to share what I know with you, then that's what I'll do. But the next thing is for me to talk to him."

Stetson sat beside his boss, Priti. Across from them, behind his desk, was Rasmussen, the Chief Security Officer, who sat still, hands folded on the desk, his large, bald head unmoving.

"I told him to use the A.I.," Priti said. It was the third time she'd uttered the phrase.

"He may have to," Rusmussen said, his face remaining so calm that only the lips surrounded by the goatee moved. "It's quite an accusation to make against the Chief Operating Officer."

"This has nothing to do with the investigation assigned," Priti said.

"It's a probability," Stetson said. "I think Barker is using data separation between the church and the corporation to provide cover from the A.I. while he escapes to an independent zone."

"Where is he now?" Rasmussen asked.

"He spent the weekend at the church retreat center with his family. He planned for the absence, requesting the approval well in advance. The stated reason was celebrating with his family after their son's opt-in. By traveling from the arena to the retreat, the flight raised no flags raised."

"Has he ever gone there before?" Priti asked, her eyes blazing at him from their dark shadows.

"Yes, every year, sometimes more often, reaching back to when Ilasha was born."

"So then it is nothing. It's normal behavior, and you are over-stepping our authority."

Rasmussen tapped a finger on his desk, which got Priti's attention.

Turning to his boss, Stetson said, "I realized on Saturday that the A.I. would review his movements, anyway, because of his rank. He couldn't have just gone there, or a team would check on him. Of course, the church safety team would stop our team at the gate, but it would raise flags."

"Of course," Priti said. "That's how it's designed to work. You make my point."

Stetson looked back at Rusmussen. "I looked at his former associates, and noticed that Barker's father worked for a billionaire before incorporation, a Silicon Valley guy named Filmore who owned the most desirable real estate in California. The data was not overwhelming, but it seemed like they were family friends. After incorporation, Barker's father was an executive with R1 for years until he died in the Collective Bombing."

"What does that have to do with anything?" Priti asked.

"Filmore built a city for himself in the Sierra Nevada foothills. He was one of the first to go independent when the unrest started."

"A dragon's lair," Rasmussen said.

"But that still makes little sense," Priti said. "How would he go from the church retreat to an independent zone without raising flags? He can't just fly his personal robo-van there."

Stetson nodded, waiting a moment to let the question sink in. "Filmore's independent zone had an arrangement with the church. Again, the data is thin, but I think Filmore donated the land for the retreat center. There is a regular flight that goes between the retreat center to Filmore's independent zone, an arrangement made early after incorporation, and the corporation approved the contracts. It's a convenient way to resupply the dragon's lair. The church gains access to commodities the corporation bans, and passengers may travel to the retreat center for spiritual reasons."

"I've never heard such a thing," Priti said.

"The contract is old. There have been no reasons to question it."

"But why would he go?" Priti asked.

Rasmussen rapped a knuckle on his desk. "When is the next flight?"

"The incoming landed at the retreat this morning," Stetson said. "The return flight is this afternoon after it takes on passengers and refuels."

Rasmussen closed his eyes and frowned, the first revelation of his thinking. "You don't have intent, you don't have an act."

"There's no motive," Priti blurted. "They are going to Heaven. Why would they do this, instead?"

"Heaven is guaranteed to no one," Stetson said. "Filmore's lair is the next best thing."

"It's still just a theory," Rasmussen said. "What makes you think they're attempting this?"

"My firsthand observation of Abel and Leah Davidson. They're upset, and there's nothing else to explain it."

"I wish we had a red flag from A.I.," Rusmussen said. "I just can't intercept a flight because two teenagers quarreled."

"The contract allows random inspections," Stetson said. "No reason needed. It just hasn't been done in fourteen years."

# # # #

Leah awoke to find her mother and sister behaving like nothing was wrong with the world. They did not know what she was feeling, and no one asked.

Her father would have been at the office for hours already. Not that that mattered. He wasn't someone she could talk to about what she was feeling just then.

She tried to journal. That's what Jaylend had been teaching her, to use the act of writing in a journal to understand what she was feeling. Choose words. Draw them on the page. Pay attention to her reactions. Use those reactions to choose more words, and on and on.

Sitting in her room, she couldn't help but stare at her computer, waiting for a signal that Abel wanted to talk to her. They had spoken every day for years, even if it was just to say hello. Now it had been once in two weeks.

Of course, they had never discussed their feelings and not about each other, so Leah didn't know what Abel thought about her.

Maybe all that bothered her was that she'd expected to learn what he thought about her soon. Now she didn't know when that would be.

Would he change his mind before she found out?

She had to get out of the room.

What she wanted was to speak to Jaylend. But without an appointment, she didn't know how to reach her.

She could leave a note at the cafe, but she wouldn't get a response for a day, and then it would be another day before they could meet. That was useless.

Leah took her journal, left the apartment, and climbed the stairs to the roof.

Because her father was a vice president at R1, they had the apartment at the top of the building. She understood it wasn't as luxurious as the apartments of top executives, but it meant they had access to the roof because her father often used robo-vans to travel.

The stairs opened to the landing pad. The rest of the roof had mechanical protrusions, solar panels, and exhaust fans. Leah closed the door and leaned against it, shaded from the sun, and hugged her knees.

She didn't feel the need to journal because she understood her feelings. She looked out over the city. To the west, there was an ocean. To the east were mountains and the sun climbing higher in the sky.

To the south was family valley. In the north, wild areas and forbidden zones.

She cared nothing about any of them.

She only cared about Abel.

Whether or not he cared about her, she wanted to see him again.

She was going to figure out how to do that. Somehow.

# # # #

Stetson waited at the airfield, standing outside on the tarmac alone. He took in the smell of oil and jet fuel, the heat rising from the concrete, and the view of the sky unencumbered by the bland and repetitive buildings the corporation had built everywhere else in the city.

His boss was there, but in the Operation Command Center the team had established in the hour since they gave the order to intercept the flight. She had pestered him about how to explain this gross miscalculation, once it was revealed, and made several threats to his career.

Being correct would not mean much of anything. Not in this world. His DNA was common. His connections from before incorporation were scattered beyond his reach or, more likely, gone.

All that he had was the opportunity to investigate. If he was wrong, the best that he could hope for would be an assignment to the investigation intake unit, where he would enter petty suspicions into the Investigation Wizard for eight hours a day, five days a week. His boss, however, would find some violation of the terms of service, and send him to Family Valley.

A combat team in an armored van drove around the building and onto the tarmac, near the airstrip. Then another, and a third. The security officers took up positions, spaced apart to defend against explosives.

A plane appeared in the sky. Three roto-copters accompanied it. Above them, two fighter jets circled.

The plane was built for cargo. The fighter jets would have intercepted the cargo plane and commanded it to turn around. If it refused, they would have cited their rights under the terms of the contract in effect, and destroyed the plane.

The plane landed, heaving from side to side in the wind, and bouncing with the weight of its load. It came to a stop and the jet engines fell silent.

The security officers boarded the plane and evacuated the pilots. The cargo doors opened as another vehicle approached. This would be the Security Inspection team. They had no weapons but wore padded armor.

After a few minutes on the plane, the inspection team emerged with the Barker family, all four of them.

They loaded the family into one of the armored vans which sped off, accompanied by one other van.

As Stetson made his way back into the building, he glanced over at Priti, but she kept her gaze averted.

Stetson had imagined a few things he might say to her, depending on what comment she made. He preferred her avoidance.

Stetson wasn't proud of catching the Barkers, nor did he take any pleasure in their demise.

He only felt a sense of satisfaction in seeing the results of his investigation. He cared nothing about the morality of their actions, or the corporation's enforcement of the terms of service.

Caring nothing about the very fiber of society worried him. And he didn't know what to do about it.

CHAPTER EIGHT

After two days in bed, Leah's cursive writing lesson was the thing that got her up.

"All done sulking?" her mother asked.

But Leah hadn't been sulking. She'd been writing in her journal, trying to make sense of why Abel had told her he was leaving the city.

Besides, it's not like she missed anything while staying in her room. Her father had been at work these past two days. Her mother and sister sat on the sofa watching stories. They only noticed Leah's absence at meals.

No one called to check on Leah, either.

Leah had few friends. She had never connected with any of the other teenagers she met except for Abel. Even Novalee Whitehead, who lived down the hall, and was just a year older, disliked Leah. It might be because Novalee's father reported to Leah's father, or it might be because Karas treated Novalee like one of the staff, and ignored her at the church youth group.

Leah didn't care about her standing in the church

youth group pecking order. She wouldn't hang around with people she didn't like just to avoid being alone.

She liked Abel, and that had been fine. Until now.

Now she was eager to talk to Jaylend.

Leah left early for her lesson and took the train south towards Old Town.

Leah's mother had agreed to the cursive lessons, indulging Leah's interests without question. Her mother never challenged her on anything, but neither did she take an interest. When Leah first started taking lessons, it had been her father who took her to the cafe and waited during the lesson. Never her mother.

Decker's Cafe was in the middle of a commercial building, with former storefronts on either side, and two floors of office space above them. At least, that's how Jaylend had explained its history to Leah.

There were signs of decay at the edges of the building, but the inside was clean. It smelled of coffee and baked goods. Being here made her happy.

A young man and woman were at one end of the cafe playing guitars and singing, which Leah heard in snippets as people went in and out of the door.

Jaylend, a little older than Leah's mother, sat in the corner, just past the large window overlooking the street. She wore a purple dress with long sleeves. Her skin was fair and healthy looking, with tan lines around the neck. She gathered her brown hair, streaked with gray, in a bun.

Jaylend gave the lessons to earn credits, allowing her to purchase food and supplies she couldn't otherwise get in the unincorporated area. Leah thought there was more to Jaylend than cursive writing. There was more to her than the stories of how things were before the incorporation. There was more to her than the complaints about how the corporation treated opt-outs, and how those banished to live out their days in Family Valley suffered.

"I'm so glad to see you," Leah said. "I need this."

"Oh my," Jaylend said as Leah approached. "Have you heard any more about Abel?"

"They're at the church retreat center, still so I can't even message him."

Jaylend looked down at her tea.

Leah sat down and leaned across the table. "Did you hear something?"

"Just a rumor," Jaylend said.

"What did you hear? Please tell me."

"It's nothing," Jaylend said. "People talk here in Old Town and it's not always true."

"Just tell me. Please."

Jaylend glanced around the cafe and then out the window. There was black Security van parked across the street, and a security officer stood on the corner.

"The corporation took the family into custody," Jaylend whispered. "It's just a rumor, though."

Leah shook her head. "No, they went to the retreat center. His father is the chief operating officer. Nothing like that would happen to them."

"I'm sure it's fine."

"Fine?"

"Please keep your voice down," Jaylend said.

Leah knew that Jaylend was right: outbursts drew attention, and attention was not good. The patrons in the cafe minded their own business though, except for an older white man in the corner. He'd been looking at them and turned his head when Leah noticed him.

"But they would never violate their opt-in agreement," she whispered.

"I'm sorry," Jaylend said. "This was selfish of me. The rumor upset me, and I thought you might have heard, either from Abel or maybe something your father said."

Leah shook her head. No one had told her anything because there was nothing to tell. The Barkers were on a retreat. "They're going to heaven," she said. "They want for nothing."

"You're right."

"What else did you hear?"

Jaylend stirred her tea and then pushed the cup to one side. "They were trying to escape, leaving the incorporated area without permission."

"I have to go talk to my father," she said and hurried toward the door.

Jaylend caught her in the doorway, handing Leah her journal. "You left this."

"Thank you."

"Remember, you can't reveal that you know anything, not even a rumor."

Leah looked toward the train platform, where two people waited. A security officer watched her from the corner. There was another across the street, near the black van.

Leah smiled at Jaylend. "It's fine. I know what to—"

"Is there a problem," a security officer asked. He approached from the opposite direction from the train platform.

"Everything is fine," Leah said.

Jaylend backed against the cafe door. The other two security officers, their faces hidden behind visors, closed in.

"No," Leah exclaimed. She turned to face the officers and tried to keep herself in front of Jaylend. "Everything is fine."

"You seemed upset."

"I almost forgot my journal," Leah said, and held it

aloft. "My mother would have been angry if I lost it."

"Do you know that woman?" the officer asked.

"She's my teacher," Leah said. "And I care about her very much."

The officer raised his rifle, aiming at Jaylend.

Leah stepped in front of Jaylend, in the line of fire. "Please leave us alone."

The three security officers paused for a split second. The lights in their visors flashed, and they seemed to relax.

"Good day to you," the officer said.

"And also to you," Leah replied.

When they had walked away, Leah relaxed.

"Thank you," Jaylend whispered.

They opened the door to go back into the cafe. The man Leah noticed earlier was standing there, holding a metal box in the palm of his hand. He stepped aside to let them pass without looking at them, as he kept his focus on the security officers making their way back toward New Town.

Leah Davidson arrived home and slumped down the wall inside the apartment, sobbing. It would have been nice if her mother or anyone had comforted her, but she was just glad to be home.

Once she got her breathing under control, she went to her room to sit in quiet solitude with her journal, but her sister, Karas, was there using Leah's computer.

"Get out of here," Leah said, clutching the journal to her chest. "Use your own computer."

"I need to look at something that's blocked," Karas said without taking her eyes from the screen. She snapped and waved through a web app, using finger flicks to scroll through text and pictures on the screen.

Leah stashed her journal beneath the mattress,

watching Karas. "I want to be alone."

Karas gasped. "Holy fuck of fucks," she said. "You want to see your boyfriend?"

"What?"

On the screen, it showed the Barkers in several images, their faces blurred but recognizable. Security team officers led them into a building.

"Where are they?" she asked, her voice quivering.

"That's Human Resources," Karas said. "They're screwed."

"Oh damn."

"Ashton told me. You know how the church monitors that stuff."

"What's going to happen?"

Karas shrugged. "Maybe Dad will become Chief Operating Officer."

Leah yanked the computer out of Karas's hands. "If it can happen to them, it can happen to us."

# # # #

Leah's mother was in the kitchen, snapping through pictures on her computer, and didn't look up when Leah entered.

Leah waited, positioning herself on the other side of the computer so that she'd be noticed in her mother's peripheral vision.

"What is it?" her mother asked, glancing away from her computer long enough to let Leah know she was listening.

"I have a question."

Her mother glanced at her again, but continued clicking.

"It's personal," Leah said.

Her mother blinked. Leah knew that, had she not been in front of the computer, she would have full-on sighed and rolled her eyes.

"Can you get off full duplex, at least?" Her mother visited with friends using a computer app that streamed video and audio between all parties, like being together but not having to leave their apartment.

Her mother clicked several more times, her breath in a measured cadence of six seconds in, six seconds held, six seconds out, and six seconds paused. She used that to show the interweb she was always in perfect control of herself and was only online to share and appreciate. No problems here.

She looked off screen at Leah and smiled. With her eyes back on the computer, she winked and pressed the off-line button.

She then closed the lid and draped the security blanket over the top. She stood without a word and strolled into the front room, pulling the door shut behind them.

"What is it, dear?"

"We need to help the Barkers," Leah said. "Security took them into custody and it's complete bullshit."

"That sounded nothing like a question. In fact, I rather think it was a demand."

"They need our help."

"They are beyond help," her mother said. "And whatever they thought they could get away with, well, that was just foolhardy. Chief Operating Officer, my foot."

"Abel is my friend. They would help us if we were in trouble."

Her mother snickered, covered it by clearing her throat, and leaned back in her chair to get a vial out of her pocket. She shook a small tablet out and popped it into her mouth, working it back and forth. "You're getting worked up over nothing."

"It's not nothing, Mother. It's evil."

"Lower your voice." She leaned forward and became still, and lowered her own voice to a whisper, saying, "You will not raise your voice in this house. Or anywhere else, if you know what's good for us."

Leah practiced breathing, in for six, hold, out for six. It wasn't helping.

"Go to your room and engage yourself," her mother said.

"I can't," Leah hissed. "Karas is in my room, using my computer, to look up information on the Barker Family."

"She's what?"

Her mother stood up and straightened her jacket and straightened the pin again. "Wait here."

Her mother left the room. She went into Leah's room, closing the door behind her.

Leah continued the breathing technique, but it didn't help. Suppressing the urge to scream, she went to her room, but they locked the door.

"Mom?" She knocked.

"Not now, Leah," her mother said. "Engage yourself please."

CHAPTER NINE

Leah ran from her apartment building out onto the street. Shaking with anger, and looking up at the window of their apartment, she bumped into a man queued for the train.

"Sorry," she said, looking at him.

The man adjusted his stance and got out of her way. His head and face covered by a helmet and visor, Leah saw he was watching something. The music was light and bouncy... a variety show produced by the church. The man hadn't heard her apology, either, as the earphones that accompany the visor were noise canceling, allowing him to focus on the show projected on the visor an inch from his eyes.

Leah backed away, then realized she'd stepped into the path of the woman waiting in line behind the man. The woman, also wearing a visor, stepped out of Leah's path.

Annoyed with the entire world, Leah continued to walk towards the woman, allowing the visor to prompt the woman's adjustments until they were next to the apartment building.

"Sorry," Leah said and stepped to one side.

The woman nodded and then returned to the queue for the train.

Leah stepped in front of the next person walking along the sidewalk, and the visor on his face flashed orange, prompting him to move. The man changed his direction and passed by Leah with a comfortable distance.

"What's wrong with you people?" she said. "Those shows aren't even that good. They're boring."

She zig-zagged along the sidewalk, forcing all those with visors—which was everyone—to alter their course. None of them even knew she was there.

They had all opted-in, of course, wearing the prescribed uniforms for their jobs, but they chose to wear the visors, removing all sights and sounds for the world, and focused on whatever was broadcast by the church or the corporation.

A robo-car flew around the corner, hovered for a moment, and drew closer to Leah.

Leah leaned against the wall of the apartment building, counting her breathing to calm herself. She'd gone too far. Disrupting that first person on the sidewalk would have been discarded by the system as an anomaly, but doing it twice more raised a flag.

Her father warned her of this almost daily as a child. "You want to be sent to the herd?" he would ask. "That's what they do with naughty kids."

What happened to people banished to the herd, she didn't know for sure. Rumors abounded, stories whispered during academics or in belief training at church. The stories were about the horrors of living on their own, no food deliveries, no running water, and no shows to project on the wall, so there was nothing to do all day. It was far worse than living in Old Town.

They would slaughter people in the herd for their body parts—kidneys and livers given to people in heaven who'd fallen sick. Hearts, lungs and skin given to the dragons to appease them.

Her stomach twisted in anger, Leah pushed away from the wall. She forced a visored woman to change her course.

"Sorry," Leah said as the woman passed by. "Good day to you."

The woman paused and turned toward Leah. The visor remained opaque, but the dance of light from the moving images had ceased, and Leah understood that it now projected her image on the visor for the woman to see. "And also to you," the woman said. She turned and continued her walk, the light dancing once again on her visor.

The anger roiled in her mind. If she had her journal, she could sit on a bench and vent with her writing. She would write about how her mother and sister schemed about gaining status, saving creds, or networking friends.

But she couldn't write in her journal, which was in her room, because her mother and sister had locked her out of her own room.

All that she could do was walk.

The apartments on either side of the elevated rail were plain and boring, repeating every hundred steps in monotonous precision. The people going in and out of those buildings, queuing at each stop, waiting to climb the stairs, were monotonous, different only in the shade of their skin. They wore similar clothes—the uniforms prescribed by their jobs—and greeted each other in the same bland way:

"Good day to you," one says.

"And also to you," comes the reply.

They smile. Of course they smile, Leah thinks. They're not in the herd.

Those projecting shows on their visor don't offer greetings, of course. They might nod to those passing by if the system recognized a greeting offered, or if the passer-by was known to the person.

After passing ten apartment buildings, the anger settled down. Now she felt anxious. She hated this place, the people, and her family.

How could she live here if she never wanted to be like these people?

She'd come to the elevated train juncture, where the spur between the apartment buildings joined the main line. In two of the directions, there were more apartments just as it was behind her, where she lived.

In the fourth direction was Old Town. Instead of the same five-story apartment buildings—bone white, without artifice, identical—there were old commercial buildings, storefronts, and apartments with rusted bars over the windows.

Old Town spread out from there, but Leah had never gone beyond the first few blocks. She'd been told there was nothing to see, and the buildings had turned to dust. The only people living there were unincorporated. That meant they were dangerous.

Within a block of this point, though, Old Town was very much still alive. Couples walked with children and pushed strollers. Shoppers carried goods back to their homes. Electric cars and trucks, their batteries charged by ancient, roof-top solar stations, rolled along the pitted streets.

The people living there had opted-out, clinging to the rights bestowed upon them from the constitution. Leah was technically one of them. Her attire resembled that of the opt-ins, but she could see others in the Old Town dressed in ensembles made of old and new clothing.

Not wanting to go home, and not wanting to continue walking past buildings that all looked alike, she walked into Old Town.

Leah walked to the cafe and looked to see if Jaylend was there, perhaps teaching cursive to another pre-opt-in like herself. There were several patrons, their clothing ranging from eclectic ensembles of long-ago fashion, as Jaylend dressed, to the full-on shabby of those with few options to dress any better than cast-off clothing.

Soon, her father would arrive home, the corporation would deliver the meal, and they'd sit down to eat. She ought to head home.

Here in Old Town, there were fewer cameras along the street. Jaylend had once mentioned how being able to go wherever she wanted, with no one watching, reminded her of the old days, before incorporation, when you could make small adventures for yourself, like hiking in the woods, whatever that meant.

"Leah?" Coming out of the cafe was Novalee Whitehead, their across-the-hall neighbor. She was Karas's age and, like Karas, had opted-in the first chance she got, but delayed her start date. She stared, now, at Leah, with her blue eyes tinted purple by her helmet visor. "What are you doing here?"

"Nothing."

Novalee smiled. "I'm doing research for a project."

Leah smiled, curious why she had offered her excuse, almost like Leah had caught her doing something else.

"Do you want to ride back together?" Novalee asked.

Leah shook her head. Novalee frightened her, seeming to love the incorporated world too much, reveling in the suffering of the unincorporated. And yet here she was, on the edge of Old Town. Leah wanted to run away from her.

"You ready?" a man asked Novalee. An opt-in, he had also been in the cafe. His visor was set to shade, obscuring his eyes. He wore the powder blue pants and blouse of the church-employed opt-ins.

He noticed Leah and removed his visor. His face was soft and round with close-set eyes. His dark hair was trimmed close to his head in the current style. "You're Karas's sister."

She recognized him then: he was Ashton Gray, the minister's son. Karas was in love with him, or so she said.

His face changed, his eyes widening as he glanced at Novalee, his face full of concern.

"It's cool," Novalee said. "We weren't doing anything."

"Good day to you," he said.

"And also to you." Leah turned and walked deeper into Old Town.

# # # #

In Old Town, the streets narrowed, bringing the buildings and houses closer to the street. The sidewalk was pitted and cracked, the cement uneven. Trees and bushes crowded in.

Along the curb, there was trash and dirt, and the broken-down vehicles seemed familiar. There was a game Leah played on her computer, and this seemed to be the inspiration for the digital world. Some cars were in various states of disassembly, with doors, panels and seats from inside the cab missing. Others seemed to be lived in, and had been spruced up with curtains.

The deeper she went into Old Town, the shabbier the clothing of its inhabitants. Many of the people she passed on the sidewalk looked at her. Some whispered to their companions.

Leah's apprehension grew and her pace slowed as she considered turning back. She had a vague idea of visiting her cursive writing teacher, Jaylend, but she wasn't sure where she lived or how long it would take to get there.

Jaylend spoke with pride about her house, how it had been in her family for three generations, since long before the incorporation. Her parents' foresight in putting her name on the deed allowed her to stay there, free and unincorporated.

There were small children playing in a park, chasing each other around ramshackle playground equipment. Parents stood to one side, chatting with each other as they watched the children.

If there were children here, it had to be safe, right?

At the next corner, she noticed the street signs and recalled the stories Jaylend told about having to learn the names of streets in order to navigate the city, before there were computers to tell you where to go.

One sign read Roadoan Road. The other, Memphis Avenue.

A woman pushing a stroller approached Leah. "Do you need help?"

"I'm looking for Taunton Drive, I think."

"One more block," the woman said. "Do you know the house number?"

"Four-three, three-four," Leah said.

"You'll turn left and cross the street. Okay?"

"Thank you."

"You're meeting someone?"

"Yes. My teacher."

"If she's not there, you'll be able to find your way home?"

"I think so." But Leah had not brought her pocket

computer.

The woman looked around. "Try to be home before dark."

Leah wanted to ask why, but the baby fussed in the stroller and the woman hurried away.

The houses on this street were set farther back, with grass and flowers growing between the sidewalk and the house. There was less activity here than on the boulevard, and many of the houses were boarded up, falling apart, or just missing.

But the house at 4334 was painted bright blue, and the trim around the porch was white. A canvas tarp covered part of the roof, and scaffolding had been erected on the side of the house.

As Leah followed the cement path through the flowers to the front steps, she hoped this was Jaylend's house.

She climbed the stairs and approached the door. She had never been to such a place. It was silly, but she wasn't sure what to do. She'd gone to other places with her family before, for ceremonies and celebrations, but those had been much larger buildings.

"Jaylend," she shouted. She looked in the window, pressing her hands on the glass. "Hello?"

A dog barked inside. It wasn't a loud bark, but she stepped back off the porch.

The door opened a crack. "Leah?" Jaylend asked. The door swung open and a small dog, black with curly hair, hurried out, sniffing at Leah's feet.

"Thank heaven," Leah said. "I was so worried this wasn't your house."

"Should I be worried?" Jaylend asked. She stepped out and off the porch, looking up and down the street. "Why are you here?"

Jaylend was taller than Leah. She wore a wrap-around dress of blue silk with a pattern of red and yellow flowers printed on it.

"I need to talk to you."

"Were you pursued? Did something happen to your family?"

"No. I just hate them, I guess."

Jaylend studied her for a moment. "Did you bring your pocket computer?"

"No. I forgot it."

Jaylend nodded. "Let's go inside."

The front room had high ceilings, a fire place, and two sets of doors. Jaylend shut them inside the room and offered Leah a seat at a chair near the front window which was the only source of light.

Next to the chair, standing in front of the window, was an enormous bird cage on a stand. Inside the cage was a parrot. Then Leah realized it wasn't a real parrot but a doll, or perhaps a dead, stuffed parrot.

The dog hopped onto the seat in front of the window, rested its head on the arm of the chair, and gazed at the world outside. The dog's cuteness overwhelmed Leah, and for a moment she forgot about how awful she felt about things. She reached out and scratched the dog's head.

"Tell me what's going on," Jaylend said. She was across the room next to her desk, which had a stack of journals, paper and books at each corner. The center portion of the desk was tidy, though, with a writing pad, a desk lamp, and pens laid out on top of a journal. "Did you argue with your mother?" she asked as she grabbed a journal and a pen and handed it to Leah.

Leah removed her hand from the dog long enough to accept what Jaylend handed to her. "What's this?"

"A new journal. A gift for visiting me."

"Thank you."

Jaylend glanced out the window as she sat on the chair on the other side of the dead parrot in the cage.

Leah realized she hadn't seen Jaylend with her hair down before. When they met at the cafe, she either wore a cap or a scarf, or at least tied her hair back. Her brown hair, streaked with auburn and blonde, flowed around her face.

In the light from the window, Jaylend's face was warm, the tawny skin looked golden around her cheeks. Her brown eyes were darker than usual.

"So you argued with your mother?"

"We didn't argue. It's my sister."

"Karas?"

"Yes. I'm not even sure if I should talk about it."

Jaylend glanced out the window. "Some things should stay in the family."

Leah thought for a moment. "I'm worried about my friend."

Jaylend's face darkened. "Of course."

"I want my family to help."

"Okay."

"When I mentioned it to my mother, she locked me out of my room."

"Was she angry with you?"

"They were using my computer. Because I haven't opted-in, my sister uses it for web apps." Leah stopped herself from mentioning the web app Karas used. Using that web app, in particular, violated terms, and one violation was all that it took. "I shouldn't talk about this."

"I know which one. The Collective, for example, publishes video of people taken away for violating terms."

Jaylend looked outside again, and Leah followed her gaze there as well. A black van, rusted and dented, rolled past. "I was hoping you could tell me what to do, but I guess I'm just being silly."

"Helping that family is a hard thing to do at this point."

Leah nodded. "Can they escape?"

"The corporation is very careful about such things. They're very good at what they do, right?"

Leah nodded again. She felt a lump in her stomach, and tears welling up in her eyes.

"The Collective can post pictures and videos, but not even they can do much more than that."

"Might they try? The Collective?"

"I've heard rumors," Jaylend said. "But when they post video on their web app, it's drawing attention to the problem because it's not something they can solve."

Leah looked up, and a sob escaped her throat. "So what should I do?"

"Your father is very important to the corporation, isn't he?"

Leah nodded.

"He's going to only do things that the corporation approves of, correct?"

Leah looked at the dead parrot and wondered how long ago it had been alive.

"You shouldn't tell anyone we had this conversation. Do you understand?"

Leah nodded.

"Okay, I don't think we have a lot of time, but I'll try to explain something."

There was a spark of excitement in her voice, and Leah sat up to listen.

"Long ago, there were philosophers known as Stoics," Jaylend said. "Have you heard of the Stoics, or stoicism?"

"I don't even know what philosophy is."

"I was afraid of that. Philosophy is the study of why we should or shouldn't do things in this life. It helps us decide."

"You mean like religion?"

"No. Religion, or what's left of it, is about following the minister's orders so that maybe you can go to heaven."

"Okay. I get that."

"Philosophy is about developing your mind and figuring out what is right or wrong in a situation and then choosing. It guides your choice, but you are making the choice."

Leah felt pressure on her chest. No one had ever discussed such things with her before. "Okay."

"Stoicism was a philosophy that taught you to understand when something was out of your control, you had to let it go and make the best of the situation."

"I do that all the time."

"Right. Now the hard part. When something is in your control, you can either be kind and helpful, or cruel and greedy. The Stoics believed that being kind and helpful was the right choice, but because it took courage and sacrifice, hardly anyone did the right thing."

Leah nodded. The pressure on her chest was greater, but this made sense and she wanted to hear more.

The dog's ears perked up, and it growled. Jaylend looked out the window.

The black van that drove past earlier had returned and parked across the street. A man sat in the driver's seat.

"You'll have to decide if there's anything you can do about helping that family. If there is, you'll have to decide whether you should do it."

Leah waited for more, but Jaylend didn't speak. She was looking out the window. "But what should I do?"

The dog barked three times. "Thank you, Blossom," Jaylend said.

Outside, three vehicles from the Security Team parked in the road, and security officers were surrounding the house.

"Twice in one day," Jaylend said. "People will talk."

"What're you going to do?" Leah asked.

Jaylend stood up. "I'm going to open the front door before they break it down."

CHAPTER TEN

Ballard Davidson, Vice President of Messaging, spent the morning composing the words his boss needed for the meeting in the afternoon. His first draft was rough, but he liked it as a starting point:

> As of yesterday, at one o'clock in the afternoon, Gregory Barker is no longer part of R1 SW. Although we don't wish to speak ill of him considering his many years of service to the organization, he had violated many policies. By the terms and conditions of the opt-in agreement, he was no longer eligible to be part of the organization.

He could have asked his eBrain to do it, but he preferred to think for himself on such tasks. He might still assign it to compare the results, but this was so sensitive that he thought it best to start with his own intuition.

Stanley Whitehead, Director of Operations for Messaging, came to the door. "Didn't see you on the train. Thought maybe you were sick."

"Came in early."

"The Barker thing?"

Ballard waved him inside. "Close the door."

Stanley was thick at the shoulders and waist, and filled the chair across the desk. Even seated, he looked to be standing up.

"What do you know of that?"

"People were talking."

"So what do you know?"

"Barker is out. That's all I know and all I care about."

Ballard nodded. It rang true. Stanley had the innocent face of a yellow Labrador, with large eyes and a big mouth, his receding hairline giving enough room for his enormous nose to not stand out.

Underneath that innocent look, though, was a jackal ready to steal the carcass for himself.

"If anyone else talks about it, shut it down. It's not a story yet."

Stanley didn't even blink. "When's the story coming out?"

"I'm working on it."

"Can I read it?"

"Not this one."

Stanley screwed up his face. "You're joking?"

Ballard shook his head no.

"When's the meeting with Viktoria? I'll clear my schedule."

"You're not invited."

"Just bring me along. I'm your right-hand man."

"I'm just using my left on this one." Ballard considered mentioning that Gregory had been Viktoria's right-hand man and look where that got him. Instead, he said, "I'll call you if you're needed."

"Ms. Jackson?" Ballard said as he stepped out of his office.

Her visor blinked, the faint glow of orange lights switching to blue, and she looked at him. "Yes Mr. Davidson?"

"I'm going to visit Ms. Olsen. I'm not taking my visor, so ring me if I'm needed."

"Of course Mr. Davidson."

The only thing that was "of course" was that he wouldn't be needed. He had dealt with Stanley for the moment and Viktoria Olsen, his boss, was the only other person who might ask for him.

The eBrains could handle most decisions these days, which was fine by him. No one ever got unincorporated for using their eBrain.

The southeast corner of the fifth floor belonged to Ballard and his Messaging team. Stanley had the office next to his, and Dunlap was in the next office after that. The office furniture in each was simple: desk, chairs, and projection screens.

Ballard glanced inside both offices to acknowledge his subordinates, but they were both in full visor mode, and the visors wouldn't interrupt unless he spoke.

Out on the floor, the rank-and-file workers sat at small desks. They were allowed any manner of keyboard they wanted, or they could use the visor's brain wave input to do their work. Most preferred the brain wave and sat reclined in their chairs with their hands clasped across their stomachs.

Some of them may have been asleep, which was fine if their eBrain was trained. And if they worked for him, their eBrain was trained.

One of his employees, Patra, a woman only three years older than his daughter, was returning to her desk with tea and biscuits. She wore her red hair up and it spilled over her low-profile visor like a fountain. She had green eyes, a small nose, and a quick and generous smile. "Good morning Ballard," she said.

He couldn't help but smile. She was flaunting her good genes, knowing she would move up in the organization.

Of course, her genes weren't just good. They were great. She was rumored to be one of the first of Viktoria's queen bees, as they were called in Old Town.

If she played her cards right, she'd be his boss soon enough. And it looked like she knew how to play cards. "Good morning Patra."

Viktoria Olsen's offices were up on the sixth floor. The carpeting here was plush, the walls were mahogany, and the ceiling was a glass dome twenty-five feet above the floor. The decorations were a mix of old and new: paintings and sculptures from before incorporation along the walls; holographs of the new art, stills and motion, displayed across the floor or suspended above the desks, designed to complement the space and lines of the room.

The administrative staff sat at their desks, visors on their heads, hands in their laps. They all seemed to use the brain-wave input but, here, no one reclined in their chair.

Viktoria's administrator, Raymond, waved Ballard into the office without a word.

"Thank you," Viktoria said as she motioned for him to sit. "I appreciate your help on this one." Her fair skin was warm and rosy, as if she'd been exercising. Her cheeks and nose seemed to glow, reminding Ballard of the beach reflecting the sun at the executive retreat.

Despite her strawberry blond hair, Viktoria's most striking feature was her green eyes. They held his own gaze carefully as he entered.

"These are never easy," Ballard said. He crossed one leg over the other and gripped his knee with both hands, assuming a protected, closed posture so as not to threaten his boss. "I'm sure we can find the right message."

Viktoria glanced at her computer, snapping her fingers to bring up his communication. She nodded.

"Did you eBrain this?" she asked.

"No. It's just me."

"It shows." Looking up, she smiled. "That's a good thing."

Ballard nodded. He'd hoped that was how it would play. "I'm sure you have input."

"It seems a smidge too soft, and then a smidge too hard."

Ballard thought a moment, then placed both feet on the floor and his hands in his lap. "How about this," he said, and then recited the revised version:

> As of yesterday at ten o'clock in the evening, Gregory Barker is no longer part of R1 SW. He recently violated numerous policies of the organization and, by the terms and conditions of the opt-in agreement, he was no longer eligible to participate. No employee of R1 SW, or its subsidiaries, should communicate with Gregory Barker. Considering his many years of service to the organization, we wish him well in the future.

"Yes," Viktoria said. "Much better. Let's go with that."

"Thanks for the input."

"What else have you got for me?"

"I prepared the Citizen Engagement report. It goes through the COO's office, so..."

"Let's hear it."

Ballard grabbed his pocket computer and waved his fingers to transfer the report to Viktoria's queue. "Church programming had a slight increase in engagement, and this has already been a strong month for them. Their year-to-date keeps chipping away at our own programming, although most of the losses are from News and Current Events programs."

"Recommendations?"

"None at this time. Church programming has been consistently on message. There are no correlating factors of concern. Eventually, if the gap becomes significant—I'd say twenty percent—then we can take a few creds from the News and Current Events budget and move it over to the Dramedy Division, which has had some very popular programming in the past."

"What happened over at Dramedy?"

"The Church recruited a couple of their best producers."

Viktoria shrugged.

As Ballard shifted his weight to stand up, Viktoria motioned for him to wait.

"I have a hypothetical for you."

"Sounds fun."

"I need a new Chief Operating Officer. If I choose you, would you recommend Whitehead as Vice President of Messaging?"

"No."

"And why not?"

"Stanley is talented and good at the rules of the organization, but it almost seems a game to him, like he's too competitive."

"Hypothetically of course."

"Of course."

"What if I gave him the COO job and demoted you?"

Ballard shrugged. "I'm here to serve in whatever role best suits the organization."

Viktoria smiled. "Let's run the message through the standard channels."

"Roger that." Ballard stood up, pausing to ensure she was done with him.

"Anyone you recommend for your old job?" she asked.

"Hypothetically," Ballard said, "Patra could be fast-tracked into the position. Direct mentoring for a few transitional weeks and she'd be amazing."

Viktoria nodded and looked away, focusing on her computer, which was Ballard's invitation to leave.

# # # #

Ballard was talking with Tyra, his wife, over a secure, computer-to-computer channel, when the door opened with a knock. Stanley leaned inside. "They're in position."

"Thanks."

"You want to watch?"

Ballard motioned for the buffoon to wait a second. "Tyra," he said into his pocket computer, "I have to go. I'll call you the second she's safe."

He cut the line without waiting for her response, taking advantage of the opportunity to remind her of his position. He waved Whitehead in.

A Security man in a suit and visor followed him in and set up his pocket computer on the desk, snapping his fingers to turn on the projector.

"It's the drone feed," Whitehead said. "No visors, but this should be routine."

They watched as the security team spread out around the house. With everyone in position, two men in suits and visors, like the guy here in the office, approached the front door.

The door opened before they could knock, and the woman—Foster was her name—stepped out, followed by Leah.

The four of them discussed something, then one suit walked Leah out to the van while the other went inside the house.

By the time Leah was seated in the van, the other suit was out of the house, and the security team hustled back to their vehicles.

A moment before the security guy snapped off the projection, Ballard glimpsed the teacher, Foster, in the front window. She smiled, looking at a drone hovering before her house.

"You want to talk to your daughter right now?" Whitehead asked.

"Just bring her here."

"Got it, Chief."

"One thing," Ballard said. "Why couldn't they hear what Leah and that woman were saying inside the house?"

Whitehead shrugged and turned to the security guy.

"Solar panels on the roof, old wiring inside... all of it messing with the signals. The sensors are spread out farther in Old Town. Not really surprising."

"No chance she's part of the Collective?"

"There's always a chance. We're sending an inspector soon to dig into it."

"Thank you."

CHAPTER ELEVEN

Leah had never been inside a security van. She didn't like it one bit.

They had her in the middle bench with security officers on either side of her, two more on the bench behind her, and two more up front.

They'd taken her journal and pen and examined them up front. One security officer flipped through the pages and used a gadget to inspect the binding. The other security officer took apart the pen and used the gadget on all the pieces.

It was a pen, she wanted to scream at them. It's for writing with your hand on paper. The stupid dolts.

She didn't scream anything, of course. It felt very much like she was in trouble, and she was frightened and on the verge of crying.

"I want to go home," she said, her voice breaking.

"You're going to see your father," a security officer behind her said. "We'll see what happens after that."

The only window was in the van's front. They drove back to New Town and followed the train platform, rolling along the pavement beneath it, towards the business district.

The security van was not in a particular hurry and

paused at intersections to allow pedestrians and cyclists to cross in front of them.

No one, it seemed, so much as glanced at the security van. It was hard to be sure what people looked at with visors over their eyes.

Leah always stared at the vans, not just when the sirens blared, always wondering who was inside or where they were going. These vans were commonplace, but still she wondered.

They stopped in front of her father's building and the two security officers up front got out and opened the side door.

Two officers escorted Leah inside. Just inside the front door, they passed through the security check point.

Leah thought they'd head for the elevators. Instead, they led her to a conference room on the side of the lobby. One officer offered her a chair, then joined the other officer just inside the door.

They left the door open and the other two officers, the rear guard, stood outside.

"Can I have my journal back?" Leah asked. She realized it was the two officers from the front of the van who had the notebook and pen.

When no one responded, she lowered her head to the table.

#

Ballard entered the room and motioned for the officers to step out. Leah raised her head and stared at him.

Good, he thought. At least she knows enough to stay quiet.

He sat down beside her. "They monitor the audio in this room," he said.

Leah nodded.

He had brought the notebook and pen with him and placed these before her on the table. She placed her hands on them and pulled them closer.

"You care to explain yourself?"

"I lost my journal," Leah said, her voice calm. She looked in his direction but not quite at him. "I was afraid I'd left it at the cafe. Then I thought maybe Jaylend had taken it back to her place."

"This wasn't an arranged meeting?"

"No. My lesson was earlier."

"And what is written in this missing journal that is so important?"

"Nothing. Just embarrassing stuff. My thoughts. You know."

He took her hand. "I'm very glad you're safe."

"Why did you send Security? I was so embarrassed in front of Jaylend."

"I didn't send them. The Chief Security Officer was made aware of your presence there, and it was his decision to find you and bring you home. He let me know, of course, but I had no control over the situation."

"Oh."

"And shouldn't you be a little embarrassed for your family's sake?"

Leah scowled. "What was the big deal?" she asked. "It's not like I hurt someone or stole something. Why did they send all those security guys?"

"It may seem quiet in Old Town, but you realize it's not as it seems. The Collective works there. They've taken executives and their family captive before."

"Nothing like that would happen."

"You don't understand enough about this world, yet. It's expected, not having opted-in yet, and still just a child."

Ballard stood up and offered her his hand. "Let's go."

"What happens to me now?"

"I'm taking you home to talk to your mother."

"Fat chance of that."

# # # #

Back in their apartment, Leah went first to her room but found her mother and sister at her desk.

"Oh for fuck's sake," she said. "Can't I please have my room?"

Her mother stood up, her eyes focused on Leah. "How dare you. Did you learn such foul language from that Foster woman?"

"I learned it from you."

Karas laughed, and her mother snapped back around. "Get out of here."

"Alright settle down," Father said, joining Leah in the hall outside her door. "Let's all take a breath and we'll meet in my office. No talking about anything until then."

Karas pointed at Leah's computer. "Yeah but—"

"Nothing," he said.

The office in the center of their apartment, used by Leah's father for private meetings, had no windows and just the one door. One wall was bare and white for computer projections. The other walls displayed paintings by artists from the pre-incorporation days.

Her father waited by the door as her mother and Karas sat on the sofa, leaving Leah to sit at the high-backed chair next to the desk.

Leah clutched the new journal to her chest, wrapping

her arms around it. When they were settled, he closed the door and entered a code on the lock.

They kept quiet as he turned off his equipment and flipped a switch on a panel next to the door.

"Okay," her father said. "This is a private meeting. Did any of you bring your pocket computer?"

Mother shook her head, but Karas remembered she still had hers and pulled it from her pocket.

Father took it and tossed it out the door.

"The fuck don't break it."

"I'm sure it will be fine." Father leaned against the edge of the desk and folded his arms. "Leah, care to explain what the hell you were doing?"

"I asked Mom if we could help the Barkers, and she—"

"That can't happen."

"They need help."

Her father shook his head. "That's not prudent."

"What does that even mean?" Leah asked.

"The issue," he said, "is that you did a risky and stupid thing, wandering around Old Town—"

"If you would just listen," she said.

"Oh I'm listening," her mother said. "All my friends are asking me what is wrong, and if you're okay."

"But what about the Barkers?" Leah asked.

"What about them?" she said.

"They fucked up," Karas said. "Ashton said Abel was acting weird."

Leah burst into tears, sliding to the floor and sobbing.

"What is this?" her mother asked. "What is wrong with you?"

"Don't you see?" Leah said, her voice shaking. "They need help, but no one is helping them."

"They're beyond help," her mother said.

"That's not possible. Do something."

"There's nothing I can do," her father said. "They broke a rule. It's simple."

"No," Leah said. "It can't be."

"That's life," her mother said and leaned back on the sofa.

Leah lowered her head to the floor and closed her eyes. Thinking of Abel being led away by the security team made her chest ache, and she was light headed.

"Sweetheart," her father said. He had knelt down beside her and rubbed her shoulder. "Everything matters when you're an executive. I don't know what he was thinking, being on that cargo plane, but he shouldn't have done it."

"Is there nothing you can do?"

"If there was, I would."

"What's going to happen to them?"

Her father took a deep breath. "My guess is they'll be sent to Family Valley."

"All of them?"

"I'm afraid so, sweetheart."

"I'll never see Abel again?"

"Not around here," her mother said.

Leah pushed herself up from the floor and wiped her nose on her sleeve. Her mother crossed her legs at the knee. Karas sat with folder arms.

Her father stood up and held out his hand.

"We're no better," Leah said.

"Excuse me?" her mother asked.

"We violate the Terms of Service every day."

"I don't think so."

Her father took a knee and looked at her. "This is not something to kid about. Even casual comments can have serious consequences."

"Karas used my computer to look at The Collective's

app."

"You bitch," Karas said.

"Anything else?" Father said.

Leah looked at the floor. "I just want to help Abel's family."

"She means Abel," Karas said. "Who is not that good looking or that smart, so I don't know why she's so upset."

"I hope you choke on Ashton's cock."

Karas kicked Leah before her father could get between them. "Enough," he said. He wrapped Leah in his arms as she sobbed. "This is serious and can destroy us if we're not careful."

Leah looked at him. "I just don't understand how there's nothing you can do to help them."

"Once you opt-in you'll understand," her mother said.

"No I won't," Leah said. "I'll never understand this."

"Okay," her father said. "I will try to find out what happened, and if there's something to be done. But you can't make these threats, even in jest, about anything we've done wrong. The corporation takes a very dim view of violations."

Lead nodded. "I won't say anything else."

"I'm not promising I can do anything," he said.

Then I'm not promising I won't say anything else, she thought, but didn't dare say.

CHAPTER TWELVE

February 1, #001B

For days I've stayed in my room, venturing out only when my parents left the apartment or closed themselves off inside Dad's office. Dad knocked on my door twice to check on me.

My mother, not once.

Karas hasn't either.

When I venture out, Karas is in her room talking with Ashton or one of her friends. She obviously cares nothing about me. Why should I care about her?

Why should I care about any of them?

I practiced playing the flute the first couple of days, but even that seemed pointless. With Abel and his family imprisoned in Human Resources, nothing matters to me.

CHAPTER THIRTEEN

Abel Barker paced back and forth in his room. The morning meal was on the table in the corner, untouched. On the desk was a single dose of Steady, unopened.

He would eat, but he would not take the Steady.

Looking back, he realized both his parents had been taking more and more Steady in the weeks leading up to the violation.

His mother always took at least one dose a day, but his father only rarely.

His father liked to drink alcohol in the evening and would fall asleep in his chair in front of the projector. That was their normal.

Now even that seemed anything but normal.

During the months leading up to Opt-In, Abel had become Ilasha's caretaker, getting her to and from school, fixing her meals, putting her to bed.

He thought it was a phase that his parents were going through.

He kept going over the snatches of conversation he overheard, trying to understand. "I have an agreement," his father said, at one point. "Can you find another job?" his mother asked some time later. "I think it will blow over," his father said more than once.

One time, Abel asked what was the matter. "Oh, nothing," his father said. "Adult things. Your mother and I have high-pressure jobs. This is typical. We'll figure it out."

"It's nothing," his mother added.

If it had been nothing, they would not lock him inside a room at Human Resources.

Even when they announced their plans to go to the Retreat Center, it seemed like a temporary thing. Now that he had the time to consider the events, there was some disagreement his father had with his boss, and a disagreement with his mother. The incident at Decker's Cafe, with the shooting, had forced them to decide, resulting in their arrest.

In the bathroom, he stared at himself in the mirror. Ordinarily, he kept his brown hair parted on the side and combed to the right, held in place with gel. Now it was a mess, spread apart in different places, twisted together in others. It seemed a shade lighter.

Stubble sprouted on his chin and in patches along his jaw line. He shaved every day before, embarrassed by the inconsistency, but he couldn't even brush his teeth as he did before, let alone shave. Human Resources was worried he might slice his throat with a razor.

Human Resources brought him a toothbrush made of paper every day that dissolved in his mouth as he brushed. No chance of killing himself with the sharpened end of that, either.

Still staring at his reflection, he saw his mother's hazel eyes and his father's taupe-colored skin. He realized the shower wall was almost the same color. Would the features he'd inherited be the only thing he'd have to remind him of his parents?

His face had broken out in blemishes around his nose

and forehead. There was no chance they'd get him his acne treatment here.

He punched the mirror. It was some kind of shatter-proof plastic, but for a brief instant it felt good punching himself in the face. It was how he marked time in this place, punching the mirror when he awoke, when they brought the mid-day meal, and one last time before he lay down to sleep.

An older woman came into his room, accompanied by a security guard. "My name is Karen," she said. "How are you doing today?"

Abel stared at her. He didn't know how to answer that without screaming, and he didn't want to scream in front of the security guard.

The woman, Karen, wore a standard issue R1 outfit, something he'd seen his mother wear every day of his life. On Karen, it looked ill-fitting, tugging in one place and sagging in another.

She waved her fingers at her pocket computer, her face gripped with frustration. "Do you know how to do this?" she asked the guard, showing him the pocket computer.

The guard, a clean-shaven man whose eyes were hidden behind the visor, helmet covering his ears, and wearing padded gloves, shook his head no.

"Just one second," Karen said and left the room.

The guard seemed surprised by this and left the room a moment later.

Abel lay back on his cot. "What the fuck!" he screamed.

Karen and the guard returned with them another woman and another male guard. The room was too small for so many people, and the additional guard stepped past the others and stood in front of Abel, his knees within inches of the edge of the cot.

Karen and the other woman unlocked a panel near the door and plugged a cable into the recessed port, and the other end of the cable into Karen's computer.

"That's it," Karen said. "So weird."

"The room is caged," the other woman said.

"Oh right," Karen said, nodding. Then she shook her head. "Wait, what?"

"It means Faraday Cage," Abel said, unable to contain his frustration. "It blocks electromagnetic radiation. Nothing in, nothing out."

The other woman nodded. "Unless you use a cable to pass through."

"The cage," Karen said. "So that's a cage."

Karen nodded and smiled, but Abel was pretty sure she didn't get it.

The other woman left, taking the extra guard with her.

"Wow," Karen said. "How d'you know that about the faraway cage?"

"Faraday Cage. I learned about it when I studied electrical engineering. That's all."

"Okay."

Karen waved and snapped at her pocket computer. "Oh, hey, look at that. You passed your baccalaureate, and you were planning a doctorate. You're smart."

Abel stared at her until she looked up from the computer. "Where are my parents?"

"I thought they told you. Didn't someone tell you?"

"Security guards removed me from the van and brought me here. Some guy in a black suit told me they violated terms of service and then put me in this room."

"Oh, that was it?"

"Counting the meal trays, I've been here about ten days."

"Well, I'm not sure what I'm allowed to tell you."

Abel nodded. "You don't want to violate your Terms of Service."

Karen laughed. "Oh, sorry. I thought that was a joke."

"It was a dark joke."

"Right. Again, I'm so sorry. Let me go—"

"Just tell me what you can tell me, okay? Don't go get someone else, please."

"Yeah, uh, we assigned them to Valley Housing, and transferred them there about, uh, ten days ago."

"They were sent to the herd?"

"I guess that's what people call it."

"And I'll never see them again, unless I go to the herd."

Karen took a breath as if to say something, but thought better of it, lowering her eyes to her pocket computer.

"Okay. That's what I was guessing. Can I see my sister?"

"She's a ward of the state and is in foster care, as managed by R1."

"Our alma mater," Abel said.

Karen looked up with the hint of a smile. "What's that?"

"It means nurturing mother."

"How about that," Karen said. She looked at her computer to regroup. "I can tell you that your sister is doing great and is adjusting to things."

Abel lay back down on the cot.

"Would you like some Steady? I'm not supposed to give it to you, but I always have some on me."

"I think they lace the food with it," Abel said. "Otherwise, I would have gouged my eyes out days ago, and worked harder at opening a vein."

"Oh, hey now, don't talk like that."

Abel looked at her. "What is it you came here to tell me?"

"Right. There are some options for your job placement, and they have arranged new housing."

"Can I see my sister?"

"No," Karen said. "I don't think that's an option."

"Can I go live with my parents? In the herd?"

"No," Karen said. "Nobody wants that."

"I do," Abel said. And he meant it. But smart or not, he wasn't sure how to make it happen.

CHAPTER FOURTEEN

Jaylend sat on her back patio, writing in her journal and enjoying a cup of tea, when a man wearing a black Security Team uniform walked around the side of her house. She jumped to her feet, upsetting her tea.

They locked eyes for a moment. "I'm Inspector Fox," he said. "With Security."

"Bully for you," Jaylend said, unable to suppress the warble of fear in her voice. "What do you want?"

Inspector Fox smiled. He was tall and broad in the shoulder. His dark hair was cut short to the scalp. He had wide-set brown eyes, and a flared nose. Holding his hands before him as if in supplication, he said, "I knocked but didn't get an answer."

Jaylend, annoyed that she found this man attractive, caught her breath. "That gives you no right to trespass. Please leave."

"My apologies. I'm not here to upset you."

Jaylend moved her journal out of the path of the spilled tea, which was making its way towards the edge. Her journal was in no particular risk, but she wanted to close it and set it aside while making the inspector wait for her response. "What do you want?"

"Only to ask you a few questions regarding the incident of the other day. I'm sure you recall..."

Jaylend nodded. "A few questions give you no right to trespass. Please leave."

The inspector took a step closer. "The questions are very straightforward. They won't take but a few minutes."

"I'm going to report your trespass now." Jaylend gathered her journal and pen.

"They know I'm here," Fox said. He opened his pocket computer and waved his fingers before it. "The tracking signals don't reach, but I'm in full record mode. You can request a copy of our discussion."

Jaylend paused at her back door. "Please leave. This is private property as defined and protected under the Constitution's forty-third amendment, and I hereby declare you to be in violation of my rights as a fully vested, private citizen."

"You forgot your tea cup," Fox said, pointing with his pocket computer at the table.

"If you're scanning for fingerprints and DNA, you'll be charged with a crime. Do I need to point out that you'll violate your terms of service agreement?"

The inspector snapped his fingers over his computer and set it aside as he leaned over the cup of tea on the table. "This is Sencha," he called out. "Very nice."

Jaylend had gone inside but lingered at the door. "Get the hell away from my tea and out of my yard."

The inspector moved away from the table. "I realize you have good reason to remain suspicious, but my official investigation is over. I needed to visit once."

"Great. Have a pleasant life."

"Have you ever tried Rooibus?"

"No."

"Would you care to?"

"What is your deal?" Jaylend asked. "Just a few days

ago, two of your buddies in uniform pointed rifles at me. And before that, they shot and killed a dozen people for no reason at all. But here you are, acting chummy, like we know each other. We don't though, and I don't want to."

"I'm sorry," he said. He took one more sniff of the tea before making his way across the yard.

"You know tea?" she asked, cracking the door open.

The inspector nodded, his hands clasped behind his back. "I was quite the snob, back in the day."

Jaylend stepped back outside. "Did you have Matcha ceremonies?"

The inspector laughed. "No, but I respected the practice."

"Thank you for leaving," Jaylend said.

CHAPTER FIFTEEN

Seeing that woman who taught cursive writing made Inspector Fox nostalgic. His own mother had been a stickler for cursive, and she corresponded with her sisters and several pen pals late into life. He regretted losing the letters she'd gotten in return, but he lost many things in the years leading up to incorporation.

He'd been working his way through the journals confiscated from Abel Barker, looking for a connection, the mention of names, something—anything—to build a case. The funny thing was that Abel had packed no clothing for the trip. None of them brought a lot because their cover story was to have a few days at the retreat. Abel had stuffed his small bag with journals.

The day before, he noticed in the video of the most recent incident at Decker's Cafe that the teacher—Jaylend Foster—is helped by a man in the shadows. The man is familiar, someone he may have known from before. Fox flipped through the journals again, looking for the pattern of visits to Decker's Cafe, any mention of older men.

He noticed that pages were missing from the journals, starting at the point when Abel would have turned 13. There were no loose pages in the collection, nor had there been any hidden in his room at their apartment. The clue didn't tell him much, but it might help.

This second time through the journals caused him to stay up very late the night before, and so he was more than an hour late coming into the station this morning. He wasn't sure anything more was to be found in this investigation, but it was far more interesting than anything else he'd been assigned, and he wanted to keep digging.

At the office, cops training their eBrains sat in cubicles. A murmur of voices filled the room, and all seemed normal as he made his way to the evidence room.

At the physical evidence room, he was informed the journals had been checked out.

"Who took 'em?" he asked the retrieval robot.

"Be more specific," the retrieval robot replied.

"Who checked out Evidence Cart 20450610-67390-C?" Fox took a certain pleasure in flexing his memory muscle for the robot.

"Priti Leaf," the robot said. "Chief Inspector, New Town Station Five—"

"Enough," Fox said. "And thank you."

"You're welcome."

Inspector Fox searched the building for his boss. Although offices weren't assigned, she was a creature of habit—like most people—and had been using the same office since their last relocation. That she was not in that office, but designated her presence as "in a meeting" while protecting her location was bothersome. She wanted to play games, so be it.

Two floors up, next to the laboratory, she was in a conference room with two other detectives.

Fox didn't wait for an invitation to enter. "What happened to Barker's journals?"

He learned the answer before she spoke. They projected two of the journal pages on the wall, and the A.I.

transcription super-imposed below each line.

"I reassigned the case," she said, tapping her finger on the side of her computer. "You can continue on the rest of your case load."

"It's my case," Fox said. "You would do well to allow me to complete the investigation."

The other detectives turned to look at him. He kept his focus on his boss.

"I don't know if the A.I. likes your tone," she said, "but I sure don't appreciate it."

"The A.I. ain't going to tell you shit about those journals. They're written by a kid trying to figure out how he fits in the world. These aren't the musings of a master criminal."

"Jones and Floorman are the best on the squad. They'll figure it out."

"Do either of you write cursive?" he asked. They shook their heads. "Did either of you write in a journal in high school, or pass notes, or even keep a diary?"

"What's high school?" one of them asked.

Fox chuckled. "Sorry, but that would be funny if you weren't serious."

"They'll be fine," his boss said. "You're excused."

"Are they going to fill in the blanks when the A.I. can't read the writing?"

"The A.I. will figure it out."

"No, it won't. I tested it already. That was the first damn thing I did. Whoever built the A.I. didn't care enough about handwriting to teach it. Handwriting is personal. People take shortcuts, scribbling half the time. Now if the kid was using Mandarin glyphs, or goddam kanji, I'd say sure, let the A.I. try to work it out."

"I still don't like your tone."

Fox glanced up at the ceiling. "May the A.I. recognize

that my passion stems from my interest in this case, and my propriety from the fact that I am the only person on the force who writes in cursive, and was once a practitioner of shorthand notation, and am one of the few people left on earth who can do this."

His boss drummed her fingers on the side of her computer. "Anything else you'd like to proclaim to me, your teammates and the A.I.?"

"He's going to mention his degree in forensic accounting," one detective said.

"And the law degree," the other scoffed.

"Here's something," Fox said. "I was a notary public, back when such things mattered."

"What the hell is a notary public?" his boss asked.

CHAPTER SIXTEEN

bel made his way to his new apartment at the outskirts of New Town. He caught the express, and for the briefest of moments the message flickered in his mind that he was lucky to catch it. There wouldn't be a bunch of stops in between.

Then he remembered his parents were gone and his sister given to another family, and he wasn't likely to see any of them ever again in his life.

He was sixteen and had his entire life ahead of him, was what the woman from Human Resources told him. Learn to be happy.

The train was packed with laborers like himself. Assigned to fulfillment and delivery, almost all of them wore the same light-green uniform and black shoes.

The corporation staggered the shifts at the depot and warehouse by the hour so that they needed fewer trains to shuttle people back and forth to the apartments on the edge of town.

It was quiet on the train. A constant thrum—a mix of sounds from the visor on each passenger's head—permeated the cabin. Only the wind rushing past outside, and the occasional mechanical thump of the train punctured through.

This past week, after being released from Human Resources, he was free to entertain himself with shows, music or storybooks watched on the visor. It was possible to block out the entire world, if you wanted to, and rely on the pocket computer to tell you where to walk, when to stop, and when to sit down.

You wouldn't have to think about anything if you didn't want to.

But there was nothing he wanted to see, hear or read.

He was trying to not use his SteadyPen, but the urge was great. In fact, he used most of his thinking to focus on breathing and avoiding the pen.

Even now on the train, he noticed when the men and women all around him moved one arm to a pocket and then pressed the tip of the pen against their throat. Packed in as they were, most people injected themselves in the throat, an easy, quick hit needing little pressure, their visored heads still, almost as if they did not know what was happening.

At work it was the same, people walking back and forth, following the robots and shifting the computers held in their hands just long enough to free one hand and stab themselves. That's how they got through their day.

Abel wore his visor, but he kept it on pass-through mode, listening to the surrounding sounds. It all seemed new, the whir of the robots, the thrum of visors, and the mechanics of the warehouse echoing in the space.

To use the pen and the visor would be to surrender to his fate, and Abel wasn't ready for that yet.

Exiting the train, he was caught in the flow. It didn't matter that his visor wasn't guiding his steps because the mass of people directed his movement. It thinned out with each building until, as he turned the corner for his own building, he could walk on his own and almost enjoy it.

As he approached the entrance to his apartment building, Inspector Fox opened the door and held it for him.

"What?" Abel asked.

"I have to talk to you about your journals."

The apartment was tiny and the only place to sit was in the dining room in front of the projector on the wall. Abel had yet to turn it on—he had done nothing in the apartment except eat, sleep and shit.

"I read your journals," Inspector Fox said. "But I didn't understand all of them."

"I'm sixteen years old," Abel said. "I wrote most of that as a child. What's to understand?"

"That's a mature assessment."

"The system works, I guess."

The inspector snapped his fingers over his pocket computer and it projected a journal on the wall. "You want to tell me what's going on here?"

"You can't read it?"

"I have to ask you about these," Inspector Fox said. "It's for the official record."

"They're journals," Abel said. "You write in them to work out thoughts and feelings."

The inspector waved his fingers over his pocket computer and it projected different pages, as if he were flipping through the journal. "Your teacher, Jaylend Foster, she read your journal entries?"

"Some of them."

"Which ones did she read?"

"She read my journal entries about penmanship and cursive writing."

"What about your thoughts and feelings?" Inspector

Fox asked. "Did she read those?"

Abel had been watching the images of his journal flip past, his stomach twisted by the nostalgia. He worried about so many things and wrote them down. Spending time with Jaylend was wonderful; she worried about how he felt. She didn't judge him for these worries; she helped him grow and mature as he learned to process the worry.

"Please respond," Inspector Fox said.

Abel shook his head.

"This in an official inquiry," Inspector Fox said. "I have to ask these questions, and you have to answer them."

Abel stared at the inspector. "What was the question?"

"Did Jaylend Foster read your journal entries about your thoughts and feelings?"

"No. I had journals for practice, and personal journals for that stuff."

"And what about the shorthand?"

"What about it?" Abel asked.

"Why did she teach you shorthand?" Inspector Fox asked.

"So we could capture our thoughts and feelings as quickly as possible, before they left us."

The inspector paused. He was looking toward the projected journal pages, but he didn't seem to be reading them. Abel didn't want to look up. He didn't want to see his writing again.

"Why did she teach you non-standard shorthand?" he said at last.

"I didn't know there's a standard."

"Did she ever say why she taught you a unique shorthand notation, unlike any other that has been used?"

Abel shook his head. "No."

"When you were at Decker's Cafe, did anyone else

ever speak with you?"

"Leah did. She had lessons either before or after mine."

"Did any of the unincorporated ever speak with you?"

"No," Abel said.

"Was Jaylend Foster part of The Collective?"

"What's The Collective?"

"Did she ever recruit you to take part in any activity that resists or subverts the management of R1 Corporation?"

"No."

The inspector turned off the projection. "Thank you for your time."

"Sure," Abel said. "We should do this more often."

"Mind if I use your toilet?"

The question caught Abel off guard. "Fine."

The inspector stood up but stayed where he was. He took a device out of his pocket and pressed a button on it. It was like the one his father had.

"This is off the record," Inspector Fox said. "I can try to get your journals returned."

"What?"

"From our evidence room," Inspector Fox said. "I may be able to sneak them out, if you want them?"

Abel hesitated. This was more unexpected than the toilet request. "I don't know. What would I do with them?"

"I just thought they may bring you some comfort."

"Maybe, but I don't even know where I would keep them. Cleaners are in here once a month, right?"

"It was just a thought."

"If you want to help, connect me with my parents, or even my sister?"

The inspector shook his head. "Sorry. That's way above my pay grade."

"So what is this?" Abel asked. "Why are you bringing this up? Won't you get sent to Family Valley?"

"I feel bad, I guess," he said. "I'm sorry, is what I'm trying to say."

"Okay, well," Abel said, "the toilet is back there."

"I don't need it," the inspector said. "I was just buying time, because the A.I. will compare my recording and my movement out on the street."

They stared that way for a full minute. Abel had no intention of offering this security officer anything else.

"I'll leave you to whatever it is you do here in the evening," the inspector said.

"I do nothing except grieve for the loss of my family."

CHAPTER SEVENTEEN

The knock on the front door was light. Almost tentative. Jaylend looked through the sidelight. The inspector stood back several feet off the front steps, dressed in normal clothes. Not an outfit purchased through R1, but slacks, a mock turtleneck, and sneakers on his feet. Clothing pulled from the bins in one of the Old Town shops.

"Inspector Fox?" she asked from the doorway. "To what do I owe the pleasure? Is this an undercover operation?"

He pointed at the steps where a small cloth satchel sat. Atop it was a blue fountain pen.

Jaylend leaned forward for a closer look. "If I take the bait, will a net fall on my head?"

He shook his head, at a loss for words. "Just, uh, a gift."

Jaylend lifted the satchel and recognized the texture of leaf tea.

"Rooibus, I presume?" she asked.

"I hope I'm not being too presumptuous."

"I'm not sure myself."

Jaylend uncapped the pen and peered inside. "Is there a tracking device in here?"

"It's just a pen."

"I didn't think of you as a pen person."

"In my younger days, I even used shorthand."

Jaylend thought he puffed his chest. "You just don't know about some people," she said.

"I'd like to apologize for barging in earlier," he said.

"Well, you are a cop."

"Please accept my apologies. I'll leave you alone."

As he walked down the path toward the sidewalk, she lifted the satchel to her face and inhaled. It was Rooibus indeed.

"I'll put some water on," she said. "Join me around back in the garden."

The afternoon was sultry, but she didn't have ice for the tea, so there was nothing to do.

"I'm guessing if you just wanted to slip me a Cosby and take advantage of me, you wouldn't bother with tea," she said.

"Such abuses occur," Fox said. "I would not do such a thing."

"Not much you can do to stop them?"

The inspector lowered his gaze. "We live in strange times."

"That's an understatement." Jaylend set down her teacup. "Is that it, Inspector? 'Strange times?'"

He shrugged. "I don't know what else to say. I thought I was a good guy trying to catch bad guys, but now..."

"You don't feel being part of the authoritarian regime that enslaves citizens with mind-control visors while banishing others to the wastelands of suburbia isn't fulfilling?"

He steadied his gaze at her. "I'd like to find something to do that matters."

She laughed. "Don't look at me."

They sat for a minute without speaking. The inspector stood and looked at the yard, studying the neighboring yards in particular. "You have a small garden, but it looks plentiful."

"It gives me what I need," she said.

"Your neighbors seem more like subsistence farmers," he said. It was true. On one side, they dedicated the entire yard to produce, with corn and tomatoes reaching into view. Behind them was a mix of raised growing boxes with beans and peas and peppers, and potatoes and beans. On the third side, that neighbor had a mix of fruit trees, produce and herbs, all packed into the space.

Jaylend allowed space for flowers and the patio, along with food. "People like to eat. I have access to creds so I can afford to shop more, but I could get along for a while."

"You have a cellar stocked?"

"I'm sure everyone in Old Town has that," she said. "What's it like forgetting how to cook?"

He shrugged. "I cooked little before."

"Momma's boy?"

"My wife cooked, and I let her."

They had another moment of silence until the dog, Blossom, barked inside the house.

Jaylend excused herself. She opened the rear door, and the dog hurried across the yard to where the inspector sat on the patio in the corner. The dog sniffed his sneakers and wagged its tail.

The inspector patted his lap and Blossom hopped onto his lap where she settled down.

"For a minute there," Jaylend said, "I thought I was going to ask you to leave."

"I was wondering if you'd worry about the neighbors seeing me here with you."

"Oh, they see you alright," she said. "There's not much else to do, so we watch each other."

She settled back into her seat on the patio and poured herself more tea.

"Tell me how you do this?" he asked.

"Do what?"

"How do you survive in strange times?"

She wasn't prepared for this. She had books, she had her journals, and she had her students, but what did she *have*?

"I'm afraid," she said, "that I'm as useful as a dog chasing a car down a country road. I teach a few kids cursive writing."

A cat leaped onto the brick wall at the back of her yard, and Blossom growled from the inspector's lap.

"You'd better put her down," Jaylend said. "She does not like Mr. Whiskers."

"Oh, it's cute," the inspector said and reached toward the cat with one hand.

"No, please, just—"

Blossom jumped from his lap at the cat, landing on the wall and leaping into the next yard.

"Blossom!" she shouted, but by the time she was at the wall, Blossom was gone.

The inspector leaped over the wall and ran through the yard. Jaylend climbed the wall and ran, calling for Blossom with all her heart.

CHAPTER EIGHTEEN

Jaylend sat on the front steps of her house, worried about Blossom, too tired to cry, and terrified that if she went inside, the dog might wander past the house unseen.

"Blossom," she said, and rattled the container of her favorite treats.

Blossom barked nearby. Jaylend stood up, and the inspector appeared at the end of the street with Blossom in his arms.

She was both relieved and furious; so much of her happiness now depended on that dog. She couldn't help but walk toward them and gather Blossom in her arms as soon as possible.

"She's fine," Stetson said. "We would have been back sooner, but I got lost."

Jaylend turned and walked back to her house. Only when she was inside with Blossom could she relax, and she cried as she held her in her arms.

"Please don't leave me," she said.

Blossom did, in fact, seem fine, and trotted off to her water dish once Jaylend finally set her down.

Stetson waited outside.

Jaylend got his gifts and took them out front. "I won't

accept these. Almost losing Blossom was a good reminder that all I want out of life is to stay here, surrounded by my books, writing when I can, and sharing that time with Blossom."

When he didn't accept them, she set the tea and pen on the ground and returned to her front steps.

"I'm sorry if I disturbed you," he said. "And the thing with the dog was just a stupid mistake on my part. I should have listened to you when you said to put her down."

"No," Jaylend said. "I shouldn't have allowed you into my garden. It upset things."

"Please, Jaylend, if I could just—"

"I'd like you to leave, now."

Stetson dropped his head and covered his face with his hands. "This is not how I wanted things to go."

"I don't know what else you might have expected for a first date."

"There's something else I need to ask you." He raised his face and looked at her with a steady gaze of sincere concern. "You can't believe how hard it was for me to make this happen, to cover my tracks and be able to wander around Old Town at all."

"Please, inspector, don't persist in this folly."

"Here's the thing," he said. "I'm trying to get in touch with someone that I think you know, and it's not part of an investigation. It's for me, because I want to leave the Security Team, and find another life, but I don't know how to do that. I'm hoping this person can help me."

"I'm sure I know no one who can help you with that."

"Tom Carby? Late fifties, I'd guess. My height, white hair."

Jaylend studied the inspector. It seemed a simple enough question, if only he were not a tool of the corporation.

"I'm such a fool," she said. "I can't believe I invited you onto my property."

"Please," the inspector said. "It's not that way. I sincerely—"

"Please leave," she said.

"I knew Thomas Carby from before. We were both investigators at the U.S. Attorney in San Francisco—"

"You need to leave," she said, and retreated to her door.

He came closer, worrying Jaylend with every step. "I saw him in the video recording, taken by the security officers at Decker's Cafe the other day, when Leah Davidson intervened. There was a man behind you, just inside the door. Then the officers received an all-clear signal and left."

"I did nothing wrong."

"That's true."

"Then why were you reviewing the video? I suppose the stupid A.I. thinks I'm part of the Collective?"

"To be honest," he said, "I enjoy looking at you."

"Of for fuck's sake," she said and went into the house, locking the door.

"Please," Stetson said. "Just one more thing, and then I'll leave. I think Tom used a device to signal the all-clear to those officers. If that's true, I think he can help me escape."

"I don't know what you're talking about," she called through the door. This was ridiculous, and she needed him to leave or she'd never have another moment of peace.

"Here," he said, and held something against the side light window next to the door. "He probably had one of these. All I want is to talk to him, and I'll do anything. I don't want to live like this anymore. I hope you'll believe me."

He set the device down on her front step and walked away.

CHAPTER NINETEEN

The knock on her door roused Leah from her stupor. She hadn't been sleeping. Just staring. Her journal was pressed against her face. There was an ink stain on her pillow from when she left the cap off of her pen. Was that earlier that day, she thought, or the day before?

"Leah," her father said. "I'd like to talk to you."

Leah sat up. She was hungry and thirsty. She'd eaten something that day, but wasn't sure how long ago that was.

Her computer had discharged. It seemed like that had happened the day before, but possibly two or three days before, as she'd only gotten out of bed to relieve herself or to eat. Anyway, there was no way for her to know the date or time.

The door opened and her father stood in silhouette. "Leah? Pull yourself together. You have us worried."

"I'm fine."

"What's all this about?"

"What's all what about?"

"This self-imposed exile. You're better than this. Stop feeling sorry for yourself. You have it better than ninety-nine percent of the people in New Town. Hell, better than ninety-nine percent of everyone in Westhem. You're not accomplishing anything."

"I'm not?"

"No. You're just wasting time."

"Okay."

"Now come out and eat with us. You don't have to say anything. You don't have to eat anything. Just sit at the God damn table with us."

"Why?"

"Your mother arranged a meal. You know how she is when we don't join her for those."

After they'd eaten, her father invited them into his inner office. "Private meeting," he said. "No computer, Karas."

"Can this be quick?" Karas asked. "I need to call Ashton."

Leah made a point of standing against the wall, refusing to sit next to her sister and mother on the sofa.

Her father leaned against his desk and folded his arms. "I helped the Barkers," he said. "It wasn't easy, but I think it's the best we can hope for."

"They're free?" Leah asked.

"No," he said. "But your friend, Abel, will stay in New Town. He's accepted a position in fulfillment."

"Thank you."

"And Gregory and Hannah?" Leah's mother asked. "What of them?"

"They were moved to Family Valley."

Leah shook her head. Her throat tightened and her stomach twisted. She slid down the wall and hugged her legs.

"Oh relax," Karas said. "What did you expect?"

"They'll be so sad," Leah whispered. "So sad."

"Maybe you can cheer up Abel at some point," Karas said.

"Enough," her father said.

"What about the other kid?" her mother asked.

"Yes, about her. Well, I had to become involved in order to secure Abel's position."

"What the hell does that mean?" Karas asked.

"We're going to be her foster parents," he said. "Ilasha Barker is coming to live with us."

# # # #

Ilasha arrived the next morning. Leah came out of her room when called and lingered in the hallway as the little girl looked at the apartment.

She wore an above the knee dress, mid-calf socks and the most expensive shoes Leah had ever seen in person. The shoes were nicer even than those Karas insisted on wearing.

When Karas stepped out of her own room, she noticed Ilasha's shoes and fawned over them. "Fuck me," she said. "Are those new?"

Ilasha nodded and raised one foot so that Karas could inspect them.

"Good for you," Karas said. "You deserve something nice after the last couple of weeks."

Leah's mother emerged from the bedroom where she'd gone to change into a casual outfit. "Did I hear you use a vulgarity?" she asked Karas. "Don't do that. Don't teach her to talk like you do."

"Okay," Karas said. "Hate much?"

"I love, you, of course," her mother said. "But we can't corrupt dear sweet Ilasha or it doesn't end well."

"And for a minute there," Leah said, "I thought you

were worried about Ilasha."

"Enough," her father said. "Let's get Ilasha settled and make some plans." He escorted the robo-porters across the apartment and into one of the spare rooms.

"Say hello," her mother said.

Leah stared.

"Say something, dummy," Karas said.

"Hello Ilasha," Leah said. "I'm very sorry about your family."

"They're not here now," Ilasha said. "I'm going to live with you?"

"Looks like you are."

Ilasha wandered into the family room and snapped on the projector as she sat on the sofa.

Karas mimed an injection to the throat and slipped back down the hall into her room.

Her mother snapped a finger at Leah. "Keep her happy for a minute, will you?"

Ilasha flipped through programs until she found something to watch. She stared, not moving even as the music started and children in the projection danced and sang.

After a few minutes, Ilasha turned her head. "Get me a glass of water," she said.

"What?"

"I need a drink. You'll get it for me, won't you?"

Leah got her the glass of water and she drank it down, then handed back the cup.

"Thank you."

"You're welcome."

"You can get me something to eat, if you want."

Leah found a bag of Sweet and Salties and handed her those.

"Thank you."

Ilasha grew tired with the show and looked around the room.

"My old house was bigger," she said.

"I knew your brother," Leah said. "We've been friends for a while."

"I can't see him anymore."

"Do you know where he lives?"

Ilasha shrugged.

"We should try to visit him. I think he'd like to see you."

Ilasha shrugged. "They said you would say that."

"Who said that?"

"The lady at Human Resources."

"Oh."

"They said I should tell them if you ask me about Abel."

"You won't tell them, will you?" Leah asked.

Ilasha glanced at her. "No."

"But do you want to see your brother? I mean, don't you miss him?"

"They told me I can't see him anymore."

"Well, damn it, did they say there was anything I could help you with?"

"You could get me something else to drink."

CHAPTER TWENTY

Three days later, at the end of Jaylend's only cursive writing lesson of the day, the young woman behind the counter at Decker's Cafe said, "Don't forget your scone."

Jaylend hadn't ordered a scone and assumed it was a mistake, but also realized this young woman, who knew what Jaylend ordered as well as she knew it herself, wouldn't make such a mistake.

"Thank you," Jaylend said and carried the scone outside.

The young woman had wrapped the scone in a second sheet of tissue paper, which was also out of the norm. Of course, this was the response to her query.

She walked down the street and sat down on the bench where buses used to stop. A casual glance up and down the street suggested no one was watching her. Still, she crossed her legs at the knee, set her satchel on her lap, and unwrapped the scone.

Between the two sheets of tissue paper was a cigarette, a match, and a cigarette wrapping paper. Upon the wrapping paper were a few lines in shorthand notation, and as she nibbled on the blueberry scone, she read, "Hompton Park, North Bench, 2 p.m."

She wrapped the cigarette with the note, lit it and puffed enough to seem like a smoker, and then worked the paper up into the flame until it was gone.

At a quarter before two, she put Blossom on a leash and set out. Hompton Park was a common destination for them. They often sat on the park benches. It was familiar.

She arrived early enough to circle the park, as usual, and then settled in on the north bench with Blossom in her lap and a book in her hand.

A few minutes later, a man with unruly hair sat beside her on the bench. He had a book with him and slouched at the other end of the bench as he read.

"That's a cute dog," the man said.

"Thank you."

"Is his name Tom Carby?"

"No," Jaylend said. "It's Blossom."

"If you're interested, you can get a nice rutabaga at Johnson Farm market stand."

"Why would I want—"

The man cocked his head, and she understood.

"Got it," she said. "Which stand?"

"Last one by the fountain. Be there at four and tell him you're interested in a nice rutabaga."

"Thank you."

At three-thirty, she took her shopping bag and walked to the farmer's market, leaving Blossom locked inside the house.

Jaylend purchased salad vegetables, a few disappointing potatoes, and a loaf of bread. The market seemed different now, because of what she'd been through, and because of what she was expecting. Shopping wasn't enjoyable in the least.

She was at the last stand by the fountain at four. When it was her turn, she said, "I'd like a nice rutabaga."

The man behind the stand stared back at her.

"I'd like a nice rutabaga," she said again.

"Pick one out, lady," the man said. "Trust me, they're all nice."

She looked over the rutabagas, but they were all dirty and blemished. None of them, in fact, were nice. She grabbed one and paid him and made her way out of the market.

As she was about to leave the row of stands, a woman came apace of her as she walked.

"That was a nice rutabaga you bought," she said.

She glanced at her. The woman was a few years younger. Familiar looking, in fact. "Mary Margaret?" she exclaimed, recognizing one of her first cursive writing students.

"Yes!"

They hugged and chatted. Then Jaylend remembered why she had come to the market.

"You asked about my rutabaga."

"Let's grab a drink," Mary Margaret said, and pointed at a vendor in the shade.

They sat at a picnic table with their drinks. Jaylend wanted to catch up with her former student, but was also dizzy with the tension and intrigue of the mysterious connection.

"I'm worried," Jaylend said. "Security mentioned that name—which I didn't recognize—and this wild goose chase happened."

"Here's the wild goose," Mary Margaret said as a white haired man sat down at the picnic table.

Jaylend recognized him from Decker's Cafe, where he often sat reading his way through the old New Yorker magazines. She'd known this Tom Carby all along, without ever meeting him. They'd nodded to each other twice a week for almost fifteen years. "You? You're—"

He nodded. With a finger to his lips to shush them, he produced from his pocket a device similar to the one Stetson had left on Jaylend's doorstep. He pressed a button and cupped both hands around the device to conceal it.

"What does that do?"

"Protects us," he said. He was a few years older than Jaylend. He had thinning white hair, and a wan, sagging look to his skin not out of place in Old Town, where food had been scarce for extended periods over the years. "We don't need it out here, but I like to be careful. We've found R1 transmitters before, and it's hard to know everyone milling about a farmer's market. You never know when a drone is lurking behind a tree."

"I just teach cursive writing," Jaylend said. "And this inspector shows up..."

"You're aware of the profile of your clients," Mary Margaret said. "You spend time with the children of the most powerful people in Westhem."

"I just teach cursive writing," she said.

"We heard about the visits by the inspector," Tom said. "Did he mention me?"

"He said he recognized you from the visor video when I was almost shot last week."

"Does this inspector have a name?" Tom asked.

"Stetson Fox," Jaylend said.

Tom glanced at Mary Margaret, who nodded.

"Of course," Jaylend said. "You knew that already."

She motioned with her head at the device concealed by his hands. "He gave me one of those because he thinks you used it to save me."

"Maybe I did," Tom said.

"Where's the device now?" Tom asked.

"In a Faraday cage."

"Good. I'll send someone to have a look, if you don't mind."

"He said he knew you from before."

"It's true."

"He said he wants to escape." Jaylend felt disembodied as she heard herself and looked at her companions at the picnic table as if she were just observing. The breeze carried with it the smell of spiced meat roasting near the farmer's market stands. A baby cried, and a man and woman argued nearby about how much cash they had to spend.

A few feet away, the heat shimmered off the cracked cement sidewalk, overgrown with weeds, as two children ran laughing toward the grass.

"Think about escaping yourself," Tom said.

"I teach cursive writing to children."

"I'm afraid he's involved you, like it or not."

CHAPTER TWENTY-ONE

Father and Mother decided they should attend the two o'clock church service so that Ilasha would be alert and energetic. In the few days they'd had her, she'd grown irritable and tired later in the afternoon, forcing Mother to medicate her and put her down early in the evening.

"She should stay home," Leah said. "I don't even think she's figured out she isn't going home again."

"She knows," Karas said. "That's why she's a pain in the ass."

"We're going to church," Mother said. "That's final."

"She's going to cause a scene," Leah said.

"Duh," Karas said. "The whole point is to take Ilasha. If your tree is growing in the forest but your friends don't know about it, do you even have a tree?"

They took the robo-van and landed on the tenth floor of the church, entering into their family suite.

Excited by the familiarity of the church, Ilasha ran ahead and searched the rooms. "Mom?" she cried out. "Dad?"

"They're not here," Mother said, and held her hand. "I'm sorry, sweetie, but you won't see them today."

Ilasha's eyes welled up with tears, and she sobbed.

Mother, frustrated, plopped her on the sofa and poured herself a drink. "She'll be fine once the service starts. No one can cry through a Cirque performance."

Leah sat with Ilasha and, as often happened the past few days, Ilasha rested her head on Leah's shoulder.

"I hear singing," Father said. "We should go in."

Leah carried Ilasha into the seats outside their suite overlooking the arena floor. Three hundred feet below them on the stage, a twelve-piece band was playing. A few people danced in front of the stage. At the evening services, there would be more dancing. If the featured performer was a well-known band, they would pack the arena floor.

Karas leaned close to Ilasha. "Are you hungry?"

Ilasha shrugged.

"Let's take her to get something to eat."

"Be back before the gospel performance," Mother said. "And bring me something sweet."

Leah and Karas walked along the ground floor concourse with Ilasha between them, holding her hands. Families were still coming in, making their way up the ramps to the arena seating.

Karas claimed to be looking for a certain type of food, but Leah knew she was hoping to be seen by some of her friends.

Karas got Ilasha a bag of Sweet Wheat Corn, and then they continued the walk.

"Let's take a lap along the inner concourse," Karas said.

"That'll be too crowded."

"I'll carry her, okay?"

Without waiting for an answer, Karas lifted Ilasha up

and headed up the ramp.

She pushed past the families bunching up along the concourse as they wondered where to sit. The Cirque performance was very popular, and all the services would be full, except, of course, for the executive suites, as executives rarely attended service, even for big events such as this.

In fact, Leah's family hadn't attended service in two months. They projected the service at their apartment, but no one watched. Even when they attended church, they often stayed inside their executive suite and watched the projection on the wall.

Near the stage, they came upon a group of kids, just as Karas hoped. Half a dozen girls and boys surrounded Ashton Gray, the minister's son. They blocked the pathway but, of course, the ushers and security teams nearby did not hurry them to their seats.

Ashton was the first to notice Karas and greeted her with a hug, wrapping one arm around Ilasha.

"Is this the recent addition to the family?" he asked.

They peppered Karas with questions and congratulations. The one person who said nothing, Leah noticed, was Novalee, their neighbor, who had been with Ashton at the cafe in Old Town.

Novalee stood back a few paces, watching the interactions, and trying to catch Ashton's eye.

Ashton stayed close to Karas, though, and also rubbed Ilasha's back, offering her some of his Sweet Drink.

With expert timing, Karas announced, "I'd better get her back to our suite. We don't want to miss the gospel performance."

Away from her friends, she all but dropped Ilasha and gave her a shove towards Leah. "Did you see Novalee?" she asked. "She couldn't say anything."

"Yep."

Waiting for the elevator, Ilasha sat down, spilling her Sweet Wheat and Corn. She stared for a second and then moaned.

"It's okay," Leah said. "We have to get more, anyway."

"What? No. Just pick her up. I'm done."

"But Mom wanted something sweet."

"Mom can go get it herself."

Leah carried Ilasha into the elevator. She noticed Karas put something into her mouth, like a piece of candy.

"Give one to Ilasha. She needs something."

"She doesn't need this," Karas said, smiling.

"Really?"

By the time the elevator doors opened, Karas grinned from ear to ear, and lagged behind as Leah carried Ilasha back to the suite.

Once in the suite, Mother took Ilasha from Leah and carried her out to the arena seats to show her off to the neighbors.

Leah was ready to give her up and sat in the corner. She wished she had her journal with her, but it was always too noisy and distracting at church services to write. Hell, she could hardly think.

Karas drifted into the suite a minute later, still grinning, and made her way to the toilet.

"Come out here," Mother said, holding the door to the arena seating area open. "The gospel performance is about to start."

"Karas wouldn't help carry Ilasha," Leah said. "And I'm hungry."

"Did you bring me anything to eat?"

"No."

"Well then we'll have to order in a delivery."

While Mother fixed herself a drink, Ilasha came back into the suite and groaned.

"What's the matter, little one?" Mother asked.

"Mommy," Ilasha said, and cried, "I want my mommy."

Mother scooped her up and rocked her for a minute, but to no avail. Ilasha kicked and squirmed. Mother plopped her onto the sofa.

"Sit with her," she said. "Cheer her up."

"She doesn't want me," Leah said. "She wants her mother."

"Well, that's not happening," she said, sipping her drink.

"I meant you."

"Fine," she said and put down her glass. "I never get to enjoy the gospel performances, anyway."

She put an arm around Ilasha and put a movie on the projector for her to watch. Ilasha, however, continued to sob and squirm.

"That's it," Mother said, and took her Steady pen out of her pocket.

"Is that a good idea?" Leah asked.

"This is for her own good," she said, and stabbed Ilasha in the leg.

Ilasha howled in shock and pain, screaming until she was out of breath.

Father came in from the arena seating. "What's going on?"

"What the hell do you care?" Mother said. "Go back and watch the show. Everything is fine."

Ilasha had rolled onto the floor and kicked at the sofa, pushing herself across the carpeting.

"It's not fine."

Karas came out of the toilet and stared. "She okay?"

"She wants her mother," Leah said. Leah noticed Karas could not hide her grin.

Karas sat on the floor and pulled Ilasha close. "She's going to be fine."

Leah looked to her mother for some reaction to all of this, but she and Father were having a heated, quiet discussion.

Karas slipped a candy into Ilasha's mouth, which calmed her as she sucked on it.

"Was that Candy?" Leah asked. She worried it was the illegal, feel-good drug Candy that Leah suspected Karas had just taken.

Ilasha's eyes widened. She sucked in a breath and then let out an ear-splitting howl.

"What have you done?" Leah said.

"Calming her down."

"She's too young for that."

"No, she's not."

"But Mom already gave her a Steady shot."

Karas, still smiling, shrugged.

Father hurried to Ilasha, who now thrashed on the sofa. "She's having a bad reaction," Father said.

"I'm calling security," Mother said. "We need medical support."

"No. We can't do that." Father was on his pocket computer, turned away for a moment to speak into it.

"What is your problem?" Mother snapped.

"No one can know we were this stupid," he said. "You're not supposed to give children Steady. You're violating terms."

"I forgot," Mother said. "It was a mistake."

He glared at Karas. "Did you just give her Candy?"

Karas nodded, the grin gone from her face.

Ilasha stopped howling, and then seemed to stop

breathing, as well. Father pressed his ear to her chest.

"She's allergic, or something," he said. "Get a blanket."

"I don't think she's cold," Karas said.

"I'm taking her to a doctor," he said.

They wrapped her in a blanket, leaving just her face exposed, and then they all went out to the landing pad and boarded a waiting robo-van.

# # # #

In the robo-van on the way home, Ballard breathed deeply as Tyra, Karas and Ilasha slept. The stress took a toll on him, and he needed sleep, but thought it best to keep his wits about him.

Ballard noticed Leah gazing out the window, watching the city pass below them. She was much more like him than he realized.

They'd gone to a friend of his, a doctor with a senior position at R1, in charge of two hospitals and a dozen clinics, on a path to make vice president and earn his way into heaven. He also had turned part of his apartment into an informal clinic, and he would see only his closest friends there, trusted to keep the secret.

Ballard heard he replaced a liver there, once, in his apartment, but knew nothing about who needed it and where they found a donor liver. He didn't believe it, but he also wouldn't have been surprised if it was true.

He shook the ladies awake as the robo-van landed on the roof. When the door opened, he lifted Ilasha onto his shoulder.

"Wow," Karas muttered. "She can snooze."

"She's sleeping off the overdose," Leah said.

"Okay, shut it," Ballard said. "Not another word about this unless we're in my office."

"Fine, whatever."

"Watch it," Karas said. "Or we may give you away."

"Dad," Leah said, "make her shut up."

Ballard snapped his fingers and pointed. "Enough."

Leah was on the verge of tears as they made their way down to the apartment. Once he had sealed the office, and he nodded to her, she screamed and cried in frustration:

"Why does she get to say this stuff? Perfect genes doesn't mean she can be an ass to the entire world."

"We'll see who gets a better job at R1," Karas said. "Or maybe I'll be the wife of the Chief Minister someday. And you know what, all that cursive writing you practice won't matter. You may as well take fart lessons, for all the good it will do you."

"Kiss my ass."

"Enough," Ballard said. "Like it or not, we're all in this together. You want to know why we have a good little girl sleeping in the spare room? Because someone in her family screwed up. It could have been the parents, or it could have been the brother. It could have even been Ilasha, blurting out the wrong thing, and the A.I. decided there was a risk."

They were all quiet at last. Tyra and Karas were both seething, anxious to get out of there and go watch some programming, or some other stupid waste of time. He didn't care what they did, so long as they were quiet.

Leah met his gaze. "What if bringing her here was a mistake? Maybe we weren't ready for this, as a family."

"In this world, we're never ready for what happens. You do what you think is right."

"You do whatever it takes to make it right," Tyra added.

"Let's just keep her medicated until she calms the fuck down," Karas said.

"That won't solve anything," Leah said. "What's the point of saving a little girl if you don't save her?"

"We don't have to save her," Karas said. "Just keep her alive long enough to get me married and you some crappy job."

"There's more to life than getting married or having a job."

"Stop bickering," Tyra said. "I'm sick of the both of you. Maybe we'll just keep Ilasha and send you both to Family Valley."

Karas laughed. "Besides, did you ever think why Viktoria wants so many of her babies scattered around? She's going to pick her favorite and throw away the rest. I don't think Ilasha will be around long, anyway."

Leah lunged at her sister, but Ballard caught her by the arm.

"For the love of A.I.," he said, "will you all please stop? Ilasha is part of the family, now. There's no changing that. If we take good care of her, we're all going to Heaven. I promise you. But if we screw her up, it won't end well."

"Shit, Dad," Karas laughed. "No pressure or anything."

"We all knew the stakes," Tyra said.

"Sure." Leah stood up. "We all knew."

CHAPTER TWENTY-TWO

In the morning, Leah's mother shook her awake. "I need you to take Ilasha to school," Mother said. "What? No."

"You can take a robo-van, but you have to go with her."

Leah scooted away from her mother and pulled the cover up around her neck. "Why is she even going to school? Shouldn't she stay here with us for a while?"

"The doctor said getting her back into a routine is best. She's going to school."

Her mother left without another glance, leaving the bedroom door open.

Leah hated the idea. She liked to wake up when she was done sleeping, write in her journal, and practice yoga.

Also, it seemed insane to take Ilasha to school so soon, less than a week after her tragedy.

"Hurry," her mother called from the other room.

Leah went to the toilet and washed herself. Through the wall she could hear music from her sister's bathroom. It was faint, but to hear it at all meant it was blasting at painful levels. That stupid girl couldn't go more than five minutes without being entertained or medicated.

There was a single knock on the door. "Are you

ready?" her mother called.

"I'm kind of busy."

"I laid out your clothes."

"It doesn't matter what I wear."

"Hurry up."

When she entered the dining area, Ilasha was dressed and at the table, staring at a show projected on the wall. Ilasha glanced at her and offered a flicker of a smile before turning back to stare at the show.

"Ilasha, are you okay?"

Getting no response, Leah found her mother in her room. "Did you give her more Steady?"

"Of course not," Mother said. "Don't be stupid. The doctor gave us something that will work for her with no more problems."

"She's sitting there like a zombie."

"She'll be happy soon enough."

Leah went to her room and slammed the door shut. Grabbing her journal, she retreated to her closet and wrote:

> I don't know what is wrong with these people.
> I must be mad because they see nothing wrong.
>
> How would I even know? How can I tell if I'm the only mad one?
>
> Should I do what I'm told?
>
> Should I do nothing and see what happens?
>
> Should I set the fucking house on fire and jump out the—"

There was pounding on the closet door. "Get out here now," Mother said.

"I'm writing," Leah whispered.

"I don't even care why you're in there. Get out now or we're done with cursive writing and that crazy bitch putting crazy thoughts in your head."

Leah scrambled to her feet and pulled the door open. "She's not crazy. She's brilliant and beautiful, and cares more for this world than you ever will."

Her mother's nostrils flared. "But I'm your mother and this is your family. Now help us out or it's over."

Her mother turned and left, leaving the bedroom door open again.

Leah picked up her journal and held it to her chest.

CHAPTER TWENTY-THREE

Ilasha's school could look like a bunch of kids playing, rather than a place of learning, if you didn't know any better. Leah attended this same school years before and, as she stood in the waiting room watching through the window, she remembered doing the same activities Ilasha did now.

In the first version of the game, they each gathered plastic blocks from a series of bins at one end of the room and brought as many as they could back to their desk. They were to arrange the blocks by color and shape to get ready for the next, and decisive, phase of the game.

The teacher projected messages that called for certain numbers of blocks of a particular size or shape, and the children raced to deliver them to her desk. If you didn't have enough of a particular block, you had to return to the bins.

The winners weren't declared winners, but everyone understood it. They gave all the children "praise points" based on the number of blocks delivered. They dedicated half of one wall to tracking the students' praise points, by day, by most recent week, and by the school year.

The follow-on game involved counting the blocks, and the fastest counters got the most praise points.

They repeated this basic pattern in every lesson taught at school—results meant praise points, and praise points meant reward.

They assigned students at the bottom of the list additional duties of returning blocks to the bins, cleaning up spills, or taking out the trash.

They taught older students variations of the same games with the children working in teams, using specialization to make use of those fastest at retrieving, sorting, delivering and counting. Leah had done well at these games, so well, in fact, that she moved to baccalaureate studies a year early.

As Leah watched, Ilasha had finished second to last in a game and was drifting as she returned blocks to bins. Leah felt pangs of concern and wanted to run into the room to help, or at least to explain to the other observers —most of whom were women her mother's age—that Ilasha was medicated and would perform better once she'd gotten used to her new normal.

Leah closed her eyes and shook her head. How stupid to be sucked into the ridiculous game, designed for nothing else but to teach children to work in the warehouse. Who cared if Ilasha was bad at it?

Karas also excelled at these simple games, encouraged by their mother, who promised she would be in charge one day.

Of course, this school was known for producing managers at R1. The final version of the games taught how to manage teams, turn a profit and maximize worker productivity. It had been fun at the time because her teams always won. Now she was disgusted.

Leah, like Karas, completed multiple baccalaureates. Leah had chosen math and physics but, unlike Karas, she wanted nothing to do with joining R1 and becoming an executive, like their father.

Leah lingered in the school's lounge after the mothers had gone off to shop, or brunch, or whatever the hell it was that they did. She'd hoped to write in her journal, but this place felt foreign.

Their apartment wasn't much better for writing. She considered returning to the cafe to write, but she worried her presence might attract attention from Security.

She'd only been venting anger in her journal since her tumult began. She was screwed.

A familiar woman entered. "Leah Davidson?" the woman asked. "Good day to you."

"And also to you." Leah said. The woman was Marie Gray, the Chief Minister's wife.

"I'm so glad I ran into you," Marie said as she sat beside Leah. "Do you mind?"

Leah hugged her journal to her chest.

"My husband and I were just talking, and we are so proud of your family for taking in Ilasha. That was an act of selfless love."

"I guess."

"It was such a tragedy, but at least there's that bit of joy still shining in the world." Marie looked over at the children on the other side of the viewing glass, then smiled at Leah. "Don't you agree?"

"I guess."

"My husband, whom I believe you have met, would like to talk to you. Would that be alright?"

Leah started to say, 'I guess,' but caught herself. "What about?"

"I assure you he has the most honorable intentions," Marie said. "I don't want to say too much. I hate to spoil the surprise, you might say. And, of course, you never know who else is listening."

Leah shifted in her chair, glancing up at the cameras in the corners.

"I promise I'll have you back in time to get Ilasha."

"Okay, I guess."

# # # #

A church Safety Team hover-van took them down the street to a church. The building was similar in design to the apartments and R1 offices surrounding it, but with an ornamental entry and a steeple on top.

"You see?" Marie said with a smile. "Just church."

The church scattered community chapels throughout New Town, but Leah had never been inside any of them.

A large marquee hung over the sidewalk announcing the performers and service times during the week. Apparently, this was acoustic guitar/singer song-writer week at this church.

"What's with all the doors?" Leah asked. Below the marquee were several double-doors.

"Have you never been to a community chapel?" Marie asked.

"We only go to the arena."

"Interesting." Maria lifted her hands with a flourish. "With these doors open, we can move three hundred people a minute. It'd be more if people were on full visor mode, but not many people wear their visor into the church."

One of the Safety Team officers held open a door, and Leah followed Marie inside.

"This is the lobby. You'll see we have restrooms and concessions on either side, allowing pickup or order placement. Like at the arena, snacks are delivered to your seat by drone."

Marie crossed the lobby and entered one of five large hallways along the wall. It opened into a cavernous space filled with seats.

"This is the auditorium. The seats have sensual feedback. People love coming here."

Marie led Leah down the carpeted aisle and directed Leah to look behind where they'd come from. There was a balcony of more seats sloping up to the ceiling.

"There isn't a bad seat in the house. I've sat in almost every seat in the house and you can see and hear everything. If there's a problem, it's because one of the junior pastors is boring." Marie laughed and continued down toward the altar.

There was a man sitting in the center of the front row. He didn't move as they approached.

"We can host almost any programming here," Marie said. "This theater has full wings and a space backstage, the grid or whatever they call it up on top..."

Marie smiled at Leah, waiting for some kind of reaction. Leah smiled.

"If you ever decide to attend service here," Marie said, "let me know what you think. I just love the intimacy of these smaller chapels."

"Everyone is entitled to their opinion," the man said. A spotlight from high above the stage turned on, bathing the man in light. It was Rohn Gray, the Chief Minister.

"I suppose you're telling me to voice mine a little less," Marie said. She held out her hand, and they touched.

"Good day to you," Rohn Gray, the Chief Minister, said.

"And also to you," Leah replied.

"I'm blessed," he said as he rose and extended his hand for a shake.

"It's a blessed day," his wife said. "Can I get you anything, Leah? We have some tea like they serve at Decker's

Cafe."

"No thank you."

"I'll be right out in the lobby waiting," Marie said, "to make sure you get back in time. Okay?"

Rohn, the minister, motioned for Leah to sit and he did the same, with an open seat between them. Another spotlight turned on, blinding Leah. She twisted to look at him.

He snapped his fingers over his pocket computer, turning off the two spotlights, and bringing up the house lights.

"How's Ilasha?" he asked. "I heard she was not feeling well and left the service early on Saturday."

"She's much better. She's at school right now."

"Of course," Rohn said. "Just nerves from, well, everything."

Leah nodded as she took a measured breath.

"Tragic situation," Rohn said. "Have you heard from the brother?"

Leah shook her head.

"I thought that was a beautiful thing at the Opt-In Ceremony, when the two of you were on camera."

"I guess." Leah glanced around the church. They suspended ropes and lights above the stage. There were dark corners and curtains. Along the wall were box seats jutting out above the other seating.

"I want you to know you can relax here," he said. "This is a church. It's a safe place. You can say anything, here. Ask me anything. You know, church property is exempt from the R1 terms of service. Of course, we have our own rules. I cooperate with R1, but I obey the commandments of the lord. That's my boss. When I see something that isn't right, I try to make it right. For instance, your friend Abel is miserable right now, and he needs a friend.

Wouldn't you like to be that friend?"

Leah nodded.

"I was not happy about what happened to the Barkers. The corporation made a grave mistake, but I don't expect to hear Viktoria's confession soon."

"My parents don't want me to see Abel because we have Ilasha."

"Of course they don't," Rohn said. "They're correct to fear the corporation. And Viktoria."

"I guess."

"That's why so many people don the visors, to shut themselves off from this world. It's easier to be told what to do, and the corporation is not forgiving to those who think on their own. Unfortunately, the visor shields them from the word of God and keeps them from doing God's work."

Leah pulled her legs up and hugged them.

Rohn reached across the seat and touched her arm. "The Barkers were correct in trying to escape. I only wish they'd informed me of their plans. I could have helped them."

"You didn't know?"

"No, my dear. They planned it on their own, and the corporation was a step ahead of them. Once they left the sanctity of the church, they were exposed, and there was nothing I could do to help. Do you understand what I'm saying?"

Leah shook her head.

"If you want to lead a full life, the life that God intended, you need to be outside the reach of the corporation."

"How? It's not like I can leave the city. I can't even walk in Old Town without being followed."

"That's right," he said. "You can't. But with the church,

you are beyond Viktoria's reach."

"You mean, join the church instead of the corporation?"

"That is one way," Rohn said. He leaned closer and spoke in a quieter tone. "There is another: we can spirit you away, instead. Escape to one of our missions, the retreat center, or hide in our community village, where the corporation is forbidden to venture. You, Abel and Ilasha could start your own family, as God intended."

"What?" Leah asked. "A family..."

"Yes, my child. You can't control your own life in Westhem if you're part of the corporation. It's not like you can just walk into Old Town and live a decent life. You're no better off in Old Town than in Family Valley. No, the church can offer you everything you need. And there's no reason not to be with Abel because you are in love with him."

CHAPTER TWENTY-FOUR

Ballard waved at Raymond, Viktoria's administrator, as he headed for Viktoria's office. Raymond flipped up his visor and motioned for Ballard to stop.

"She's so busy right now," he said. "Would you mind waiting just a second?"

"No problem."

"I've never seen it quite like this."

Ballard sat in one of the cushioned seats outside the office and ordered a coffee with his pocket computer.

Raymond, in his late twenties, was back on his computer, whispering now, and focused.

Ballard wondered why he didn't use the obfuscator to shield the conversation, but even the good ones still made dumb mistakes. If you ignore your eBrain all the time, there's no helping you.

Raymond had blue eyes and dark hair. His skin was a light tan, but it seemed he wore makeup on his face to bring in more bronze colors. He was trim and good looking, and sported a few days' growth on his face to enhance his masculinity, such as it was.

"She'll see you now," Raymond said, and shot Ballard a quick smile.

Viktoria seemed to be riding a rocket, her eyes wide

open and clutching her desk with one hand as she waved a hello to Ballard.

"This has been a day," she said.

"Aren't they all?"

"Yes, and I love it."

Ballard smiled. He'd rather wait to see what was on her mind before saying too much.

"I want to congratulate you on taking care of the Barker girl. Not too many people would put themselves out and take on the challenges."

"She's the innocent bystander in an unfortunate situation."

"Still, most people would have let her go down with the ship."

Ballard nodded. The thing he hated most about incorporation is that everyone looked out for themselves. With just a bit of forward thinking, you could gain an advantage against them. "It will be a bit of stress, but she's a dutiful child. Her genes are pretty good, too."

"We don't have to dance around it," Viktoria said. "She's one of mine. You know what that means."

"I'll take good care of her."

"Thank you."

"Any special instructions?" Ballard asked.

"Nothing you don't know, but important enough to repeat: keep her safe until it's time to opt-in. That investment doesn't pay off until she's part of the organization."

"Roger that."

"How's your daughter?" Viktoria asked.

"Leah is fine," Ballard said. "She was shaken by the shooting, but she's taking an active role in Ilasha's care."

Viktoria nodded once. "I'm holding the COO position for you. I want Leah to opt-in soon. Once she does, the job is yours. But I can't hold it much longer."

"Understood."

Viktoria leaned back in her chair and relaxed, a rare sight that Ballard found a little worrisome.

"Hartlyn is going to Heaven," she said. "I'm taking over all of Westhem."

"Congratulations."

"There won't be many changes. I'll keep my offices here. The COO here will be COO of Westhem."

"Should I work on the messaging?"

"Not just yet," she said. "You know I could go to Heaven right now, and sometimes I think I might. I believe in what we've built and I want to make sure it's not just stable, but thriving. Westhem will be Westhem in ten thousand years, and Heaven as perfect and beautiful as it is today."

"I want that too."

"Great," she said. "So we've taken these firm steps to create a pool of potential leaders, but it's up to parents like you to mold those raw materials. I need you to get them in the office, and then I can polish them."

"I want that too."

Viktoria smiled again. "If you play your cards right, you'll join us in Heaven before you know it."

Ballard returned her smile. "I've heard good things about it."

CHAPTER TWENTY-FIVE

L eah got up from her bed and paced her room. Who could she talk to? Journaling was getting her nowhere. She couldn't stand to be in the same room with her family, so she wasn't going to talk to them. But who else was there?

Talking to Abel would condemn him to Family Valley.

To just visit Jaylend would get her shot.

Talking to her parents was like talking to a corporate robot.

And she'd rather jump off a building than talk to Karas.

The minister wanted to talk, but that was weird.

She leaned on the windowsill and propped her head on her hands as she gazed out. They were on the top floor, and the sidewalk was about eighty feet below. If the window opened, she could throw something out and see how long it took to hit the cement. That would be fun. It would get her sent to Family Valley, though.

She could calculate how long something would take to land from this height. They studied this in her Physics program, and she could look up the formula for the pull of gravity, which was something like thirty-three feet per second.

Galileo had figured out gravity by dropping stuff out a window and timing its fall. He had done that during the inquisition, when being caught pursuing scientific thoughts got you tortured and burned alive.

If he did his work during the inquisition, couldn't she do something now?

Leah dropped Ilasha at school one morning and then took a train south toward Old Town. She got off at the station nearest Decker's Cafe.

She visited the vendor carts below the tracks and, under the guise of admiring the flowers offered by one of the unincorporated, she looked around and decided there was only a single security guard walking a beat.

Leah spent a few creds on old pins and jewelry, bought a bean salad to eat, and picked through hats and handbags. By the time she was done shopping, there were four armed security guards patrolling the area.

She ate the bean salad in the shade of a tree, and a fifth security guard joined the patrol before she ate the last bean.

Not wanting to take the risk of bringing more harm to Decker's Cafe, she walked to the next street in Old Town and visited a clothing store there.

It wasn't so much a store as it was a building full of vendors with carts laden with goods. The store was popular with young people from New Town who would put together ensembles from these carts, resisting the custom to dress like opt-ins who ordered clothing from the R1 store.

After her first lap around the vendor carts, there was a black van parked out front and an unarmed security officer standing near the doorway.

Leah, alarmed at what she had learned, bought several pieces of clothing at random, stuffing them into her bag, and hurried back to the train station.

She waited a day to calm her nerves before making the trip again. This time, Leah left her pocket computer in Ilasha's storage bin at the school. She also stepped into the restroom and changed her outfit, including the underwear, in case anything had been chipped by R1.

With her face covered by a wide-brimmed felt hat, she took the train toward Old Town again.

She didn't notice a security officer until she after browsing the carts beneath the train station. It was just a lone guard, toting a weapon, marching his beat.

Not taking any chances, she went to the store on the next block and browsed the carts there, picking up another random selection of clothing.

She emerged from the store and was pleased that there were no security officers at all.

Taking the long way around, she circled the block and sat on a bench across the street from Decker's Cafe. That lone security guard, making his rounds, marched in front of the cafe. When he turned at the corner, Leah crossed the street.

She'd brought paper along and wrote out a note for Jaylend inside the cafe. She used their shared shorthand notation. After a last, reassuring glance out the window, she gave the note to the clerk, bought herself a scone, and returned to New Town.

She waited three more days before attempting the trip again. As far as she understood it, the A.I. would raise alerts if it noticed her pattern. Stepping out of Ilasha's school wearing her latest random outfit, her face covered by a different hat, there was no security presence waiting for her.

She went directly to Decker's Cafe. As she drew near, she realized she hadn't varied the time of day in her visits. She had fallen into a pattern.

There was nothing to do except choose a different time slot next time.

Leah lingered by the wall of books and magazines. When she confirmed no security officers gathered outside, she bought a scone and left.

She waited until she was under the shade of the tree near the train station to unwrap the scone. Between the two sheets of tissue paper was a note, written in the shorthand notation she shared with Jaylend, agreeing to meet.

Three days later, they met on a bench in the shade down the block from Decker's, each with a scone and a mug of tea. The bench was in front of a small park, set back from the sidewalk a few feet. Jaylend got there first.

As Leah approached, Jaylend put a finger to her lips and indicated the other end of the bench with her eyes. Before speaking, Jaylend placed a small device between them on the bench and pressed one of its buttons.

"There," she said. "We can speak a little more freely." She explained what it did, and that she'd had it confirmed and inspected, "by someone who knows about it."

"Oh, I hope so," Leah said. "I don't want you to get hurt. You mean more to me than..." Leah's throat tightened, and she couldn't finish the thought.

"It's fine," Jaylend said. Her eyes were steady and comforted Leah.

After a sip of tea, Jaylend said, "Life is never what we hoped it'd be when we were young, but we can work to make it what we need it to be."

"I don't see how that's possible."

"You came to see me," Jaylend said. "We're safe, and that took a lot of work. Thank you for making the effort."

Leah felt a little better. "I'm just so unhappy right now," she said. "I don't want to opt-in to this world, and I don't want to work at R1. The church can go to hell. I realize I have it better than almost everybody, so I shouldn't complain, except that this entire world is fucked up and I don't know what to do."

"If it was possible, I'd let you live with me."

Leah smiled.

"Hell, I'd give you my house after I'm dead."

"I don't want to think about that."

The breeze picked up and the chorus of leaves in the tree above them whispered. A sparrow set down on the sidewalk and Leah tossed it a part of her scone, attracting three more sparrows.

"Now you've done it," Jaylend said.

"I want to run away," Leah said. "But I worry they may hold you to blame."

"They wouldn't be wrong," Jaylend said. "I don't want to hurt you or your family, but I see how unhappy you are. And I'm no fan of R1, so don't carry the burden of my life. I'm not saying I want to run afoul of the corporation, but I'm a big girl."

"I don't know where I would go, and I don't want to leave without Abel. It's my fault what happened to him and his family. If I hadn't tried to help that man with the bundle who got shot, Abel's parents may not have tried to run away."

"No, Leah," Jaylend said. "What happened to Abel and

his family is not your fault. You didn't shoot those inno-cent people, you didn't destroy that family."

Leah looked around, worried that security officers might be gathering. "It's so quiet and nice here, people just living, but it all gets ruined."

"It's hard living anywhere," Jaylend said. "Even you have to be careful about everything you say or do, right? That's what tore apart Abel's family, and that's what killed those people."

"I don't want to be part of the corporation," Leah said. "That's the one thing I know with absolute clarity."

Jaylend took a long drink of her tea. "It might be pos-sible for you to find a place to live here in Old Town. It's difficult living here, though."

"All these people figure it out," Leah said. "You figured it out."

Jaylend nodded. "Escaping is harder. They would look for you to the ends of the earth."

"I don't want to go without Abel. I worry about how unhappy he is."

"That will be even harder."

"He's probably chipped," Leah said. "I don't know what to do about that. What am I saying? I don't even know how to talk to him without making things worse."

Jaylend pushed the device on the bench closer to Leah. "If you do talk to him, use this."

CHAPTER TWENTY-SIX

Back at the Security Station, Inspector Fox retrieved his personal files out of the storage closet and took them to an open cubicle. He settled into the seat and opened the box, pausing for a moment to enjoy the smell of paper.

The files were from the old days, before incorporation —his hand-written notes and typed reports. He'd never been a fan of technology at any point in his life and had been reluctant to use computers until forced by his various bosses.

He was fine using computers the old way, typing at a keyboard, but hadn't quite gotten the hang of the wave and snap techniques. And there was no way in hell he'd allow the visor to read his brain waves for input. That shit was evil.

Stetson pulled out his favorite file, the notes from his years as an investigator in the Federal Attorney's Office of San Francisco. He'd felt lucky to get the job and realized he was luckier than he ever thought he'd be.

The Federal Attorneys worked the most complicated cases—crime syndicates, securities fraud, drug cartel— and spent years investigating and building the case. He'd studied forensic accounting in college and thought maybe he could catch on with the FBI. He enjoyed working with the best minds, grappling with the hardest problems, and applied to law school with a revised plan to become a Federal Attorney.

There were about two dozen Federal Attorneys across what used to be America, and each one headed up an independent office. They each had anywhere from ten to twenty associate attorneys, depending on the case load, and each one of those associates had a team of investigators working a couple of dozen cases.

On one such team, he met former police detectives, FBI agents, prosecuting attorneys and defense attorneys, all bringing their talent for investigation and deduction to bear. It was like being in a room full of Sherlock Holmeses, and a handful of Watsons, all trying to crack a case.

What he noticed first was that everyone took copious handwritten notes of everything said. Some wrote out mind maps, others wrote in outline form, and a few wrote out complete sentences, their pens moving at dizzying speed.

In every formal meeting, there were two secretaries taking notes in shorthand which were later transcribed, typed and distributed. Still, everyone took notes by hand.

Even when everyone had laptops, tablets and smart phones, they still wrote by hand, despite the meeting being recorded and transcribed word for word.

Some notes in the file made no sense to him, but several still did. His brain recalled the conversation, the looks on the faces, and the line of thinking they shared. All that remembered despite the Great Flooding, the Great Famine and the Great Revolution that had torn apart America and paved the way for Incorporation.

"You are here," Fox's boss said. She was a large presence and cast a shadow across his desk. "I've been calling you."

Stetson looked at his pocket computer, which he'd set down next to his visor on the desk, and was now blinking. "What's up?"

"You keep missing calls, I'm going to insist on an implant."

"I guess I'll have to retire, then."

"That's not an option."

Stetson tired of the discussion. "What do you need?"

"My office," she said, and walked away.

The office was no fancier than a large cubicle with four walls and a door. The desk was against one wall, and there were two chairs for guests, but with everyone sitting, their knees touched. "What'd you get on Foster?"

"Nothing. She seems to be a cursive writing teacher, living on next to nothing in an inherited house that needs repair."

"The A.I. indicates possible Collective support."

Stetson laughed, covering it with a cough. "What's the degree of confidence?"

"I'm not worried about that right now. I'm interested in covering our bases."

"You want to cover your ass."

She glance up at the ceiling. "Have you always been this subordinate?"

"No," Stetson said. "I just like to do things my way. It's Old Town, and we have limitations. I think my techniques work best down there."

"You ignore the new techniques and it might blow up on you."

"I'll take that under advisement."

When he stood up, his boss held up her hand. "Have

you looked at her client list? The children of half-a-dozen executives. The children of clergy. Even a couple of our own team. That's what's driving the A.I."

"It could just be over-achieving elite keeping up with the Joneses."

"What the hell does that mean?"

"It's old," he said. "Like me."

CHAPTER TWENTY-SEVEN

They promoted Ballard to Chief Operating Officer and his first official act was to compose the message about his own promotion because he was still in charge of Messaging. On the desk was a leather-bound journal, small enough to fit in a pocket, open to a page where he'd been scribbling with a pen.

Ballard balanced a metal pen on his left hand and spun it around his index finger, a distraction he'd learned decades before to allow his brain to think. As ideas emerged, he made a note or drew a picture on the paper. As far as he knew, he was the only executive that still wrote this way, working out ideas. Almost all the others had shifted their thinking to their eBrain.

The trick was to be humble while also bragging, putting other executives on notice that this wasn't a fluke, and they needn't bother undercut him, hoping to steal his promotion.

As if on cue, Stanley Whitehead darkened his door.

"Nice digs," Stanley said. "The extra space is huge."

"It promotes efficiency." Ballard was sincere. To him, having the proper amount of room to complete a task was key to its efficient execution. Jamming a bunch of executives into a tiny office to have a discussion would only crowd their egos, and that always resulted in stalemate.

Stanley didn't realize, but in all the years of working together, Ballard never brought Stanley into his office with anyone else. The man was too competitive.

Also, he didn't fit in the chair.

"Is this what I think it is?" Stanley asked, reaching across the desk for the journal.

Ballard pulled it away and slipped it into his breast pocket, but kept the pen out and twirled it in his hand. "It's about the messaging for my promotion. Is that what you thought?"

Stanley opened and closed his mouth. Then he said, "Yeah."

"Is there anything else, Stanley?"

"I heard the old lady got promoted, too. She's moving up to all of Westhem?"

"Where did you hear that?"

Stanley chuckled. "I have friends in Security. Did you know that? Of course you did. I started there. It's not a secret. Just not public knowledge."

"Talking about her promotion out of turn would be a problem."

"For some folks, maybe." Stanley admired the office again. "I was assuming I'd get your old job, so I wrote up a version of the messaging, also mentioning me, of course. What d'you think?"

"Haven't seen it."

"You didn't get it?"

Ballard shook his head, kept his eyes on Stanley. "Not unless you delivered it when you stepped into this office."

Frowning, Stanley took out his pocket computer. "It's still a draft. Hang on."

He snapped and waved his fingers. "There you go."

Ballard lowered his eyes to the viewing screen

propped on his desk. He read:

> Viktoria Olsen, longtime and loyal Chief Executive of R1 West, has been promoted to Chief Executive Officer of R1 Westhem, with responsibility for the entire organization. She will continue her day-to-day responsibility for R1 West. Bringing her experience in messaging, distribution, delivery and operations to the job, the Board of Directors is confident that R1 West will continue its track record of being the most efficient division in R1, and will further improve its customer satisfaction ratings to near perfect marks.
>
> Ms. Olsen began her career in R1 East, and has held several positions of leadership, consistently exceeding expectations.
>
> Her new role is effective May 1st, #001B, and is grateful for the support of her team and the confidence of the Board.
>
> Hartlyn Poole, outgoing Chief Executive of R1 Americas Division, will ascend to Heaven with his wife and eight children, and their families, including twenty-three grandchildren. May they enjoy the glorious prosperity and abundance of Heaven for all eternity.

Ballard noticed Stanley was busy with his pocket computer. "Your eBrain write this?"

"Yep," Stanley said. "Trained it myself."

That was Stanley's go-to joke, but Ballard wasn't amused. That joke never amused him. Now he was annoyed.

"I don't like it," he said.

"Sure, it needs a word or two, but that's pretty close to finished."

Ballard shifted his gaze to the R1 mission statement on the wall: "Customer needs are first. Efficient delivery is second. Everything else serves those goals."

He drummed his fingers, deciding how to proceed. He could continue to develop Stanley, or he could let him know that the job for VP Messaging was going somewhere else, or—

"I guess it needs something," Stanley said. "I'll take another shot at it."

"Try it without the eBrain."

"Will do," Stanley said, but he seemed in no hurry to leave.

"Anything else?"

"I have to tell you, I thought this was about the VP Messaging job. I figured I'd finish this message and make it the first thing I send out."

"Viktoria hasn't decided."

"Isn't it your decision?"

"She wants to set up her team just the way she wants it."

"Yeah, but..." Stanley stopped himself and took a breath.

"Let me know about the message as soon as you're ready."

This time, Stanley stood up and took a step towards the door. He paused, though.

"How's the new kid? My daughter saw her at church over the weekend."

"Fine, now. We all had to make some adjustments to routine."

Stanley nodded. "And your older daughter? Karas?"

"Fine. Why do you ask?"

"I hate to even bring it up but, you know, father to father, my daughter noticed Karas taking some Candy she got from one of the other kids."

"If she thought it was Candy, Novalee should have notified security."

"She wasn't sure and didn't want to make a stink."

"Of course."

"We're friends and neighbors, so you don't just call security on your neighbors, right?"

"Right, unless someone's safety is at stake."

"That's what I told her. I mean, Karas was carrying around the new one, so of course she wouldn't put her at risk."

"I trust Karas, I'm sure just as you trust Novalee."

"That new one is precious cargo."

Ballard nodded. He hadn't moved a muscle other than his lips to speak. Stanley had surprised him, and he didn't want Stanley to know it. Was Stanley so reckless he would say these things, knowing they recorded all audio throughout the building? Was it a single bet, winner take all?

"Thanks for mentioning it. I'll talk to her."

Stanley smiled. "Hey, and if there's anything I can do to improve my chances on getting that promotion, or any promotion, you'll let me know?"

"You can count on it."

CHAPTER TWENTY-EIGHT

Abel's pocket computer vibrated with a high-priority notification. It was from the church, reminding him he had not attended in three weeks, violating the Terms of Service. "Let us know if you'll be able to rectify this soon," the notification said.

"Fuck me," Abel said. He glanced around the train, but the other passengers were in full visor mode.

As he trudged toward the apartment, his pocket computer vibrated again. "You're only three minutes from the North Jones Street Church theater," the notification said. "Attend tonight's performance and all your sins will be forgiven."

The church was a block further along the raised rail lines, past where he would turn to get to his apartment complex. A line of people wearing visors queued outside, waiting to get in the theater.

They gave Abel a seat in the back, on the aisle, with empty seats all around him. That was fine. It had been a long day, and he needed to clean up, which he may or may not do when he got back to his apartment.

He didn't care either way how he smelled.

The show started a few minutes late. A three-piece band sang songs of gratitude about the abundance of

God's world, but the congregation was unruly, talking among themselves.

The ushers walked up and down the aisles and used lasers to get the attention of those talking. Soon, the crowd was clapping in rhythm with the music. Those not clapping were busy with their pocket computers, which was fine with the ushers—and God.

They brought the lights up for the first abundance testimonial. As the ushers patrolled the aisles, Abel wondered at the purpose of forcing people to attend church, then having to force them to pay attention. The larger churches had better performers, of course, and the ushers weren't needed to hold the congregation's attention.

When they lowered the lights for the next musical performance—a six-piece band playing traditional rock hymnals—an usher sat a congregant next to Abel.

"Sorry," she said.

Abel recognized the voice. It was Leah.

"Hey," he whispered. In the low light, he couldn't quite believe he saw her right beside him.

"Don't worry," she said. "You won't get in trouble. It's been arranged."

"Okay," he said. "At this point..."

She took his hand and stroked his palm, using their shorthand notation.

"I'm not happy with how things are," she wrote. "Are you?"

"No," he replied. "Miserable."

"I think we should try to leave this place."

"Go where?" he asked.

"Old Town. Our Friend there will help."

"Are you sure?"

She wasn't, but she made it clear she didn't want to go on like this. "We have to try."

He agreed, but if his parents couldn't figure it out, how could they?

She explained about the offer from the church, but she didn't trust the minister. "Too many rumors," she wrote.

Abel nodded. "What then?"

She lifted something from her lap: a device like his father had to obfuscate their conversation.

"This may help you?" she wrote. She passed the device to him and he slipped it into his pocket.

CHAPTER TWENTY-NINE

Ballard's pocket computer vibrated, then his wrist computer lit up, and then his visor flashed from the corner of his desk.

The message on his pocket computer was from his boss, Viktoria: "We need to talk."

"Ms. Jackson," Ballard called through his open door as he gathered his things. "Is there anything I need to know about?"

She appeared in the doorway, her visor covering her eyes. "No, sir. Things seem normal."

"Has my family tried to reach me?"

"No, sir."

Ballard stepped past her. "I'm going up a floor."

"It's Whitehead," Viktoria said as she also stood up. "The horse's ass requested a transfer to Security Service."

"He'd start over?"

"It turns out he has a couple of friends there, and can manage a lateral. They'll give him a few extra credits."

"That would put him fairly high up?"

Viktoria nodded. "You know Rasmussen thinks he should run this place. If that talking horse gives him any data at all, it'll be an expensive pain in my—"

Her computer chirped, and she glanced at it. "Is everything alright with your family?" she asked.

"I've heard nothing to the contrary."

"Ilasha, your ward, was left at her school past pick up time."

"Oh, no."

"Twelve minutes."

Ballard pulled his pocket computer and waved his hand above the controller, drilling into the data.

"Your youngest picked her up. They should be home now."

Ballard set the computer aside. "Good. I'm so very sorry—"

Viktoria held up a hand. "But they aren't home yet. They seem to be headed toward Old Town."

Ballard's throat tightened. He wanted to shout in anger but that would be the last thing he did at R1. What mattered now was his reaction. Panic, and he was done for.

"I'd like to take care of this and ensure it never happens again."

"I'd like you to do that, as well."

On the way back to his office, Ballard queued up the self-destruct program on his computer and set his thumb in place to launch it. It was possible a security team would be waiting.

Ms. Jackson looked at Ballard as he approached.

"I need a few minutes of privacy," he said.

"Of course, Mr. Davidson."

With the door locked, he dequeued the self-destruct program and ordered a robo-van.

It would be three minutes before he could board it, so he contacted Tyra.

"Where are you?" he asked.

"I'm volunteering at The Human Humane Society."

"Who was supposed to pick up Ilasha?"

"One of the girls, I suppose."

"They were late."

"What? Oh. Okay."

"Viktoria was notified, and it's a problem."

"Shit. Okay."

"Leah has her now, and she's gone off-route."

"What the hell for?"

"All that matters is we get them home. I'm sending you their tracking code."

"Okay, but aren't you going for them?"

"Yes. Every second counts with this one. First one there gets them home."

Ballard didn't want to spook Leah into running, so he directed the robo-van to a point just ahead of them. He caught a glimpse of them as the robo-van descended. Leah held Ilasha's hand as they strolled. There was no particular urgency, and they had snack bags.

Most important was that there were no security guards paying attention to them.

"Leah," he called out. "Everything okay?"

She stopped and looked, staring as he approached.

Ballard kneeled and placed a hand on Ilasha's head. "How about you, tumbleweed? Are you okay?"

Ilasha nodded.

Leah continued to stare.

"You're not surprised to see me?" he asked.

Leah shrugged and looked up and down the corner

where they stood, then up at the top of the buildings.

Ballard stood up and placed a hand on Leah's shoulder. "Let's go home."

CHAPTER THIRTY

Inspector Fox sat at a desk at the Security offices, struggling to translate Abel Barker's shorthand notation. This began as idle curiosity to see if he could remember how it worked, but grew into an intellectual challenge, something he'd been subconsciously craving.

It frustrated him, however, and tied his stomach in a knot. He persisted because the frustration was about many things in this world.

The main thing about shorthand he remembered was the warning offered by his first instructor many years ago, to beware "griffonage," illegible handwriting, and that if your work was so sloppy that you struggled to interpret it, you were defeating the purpose of shorthand notation.

Had his boss confronted him during his frustration and accused him of insubordination, he wouldn't have argued. That's how stupid he felt.

This morning, however, he awoke with an inkling of meaning for some shapes in the journal. He hurried in to access the secure images of the journal, and began perusing them, feeling like he knew what they meant.

The frustration eased a bit when he used his own pen to mimic the strokes digitized and projected. Now he kicked himself for not using this technique when he held the journals in his hand, certain that the feel of paper, the weight of the pen, and the motions would trigger the memories.

He deciphered a smattering of strokes and was overcome by a mix of joy and sadness. It reminded him of how hopeful and happy he'd been back when he took this training in shorthand—with the Teeline system. He looked forward to an interesting life. He thought he might make a difference in the world.

Who could have guessed that the "interesting" part of life would be the cascade of natural disasters, fires, tornadoes and hurricanes making great swaths of the country uninhabitable? Making a difference became "surviving."

The rising oceans swallowed entire cities. It reduced Florida to a strip of land before being abandoned, and all the bordering States were so consumed by their own problems they didn't bother to annex what remained.

The return of various diseases, war with Canada, and Mexico going dark sparked chaos and tribalism.

Two hundred million Americans died in six years. Still, it was one of the luckiest countries on the planet. The Middle East, Northern Africa, and much of South Asia were uninhabitable and presumed void of all human activity. The same was probably true of Central and South America, but there had been no reports about anything not on the coast which was being colonized by R1.

What remained in North America of the government, infrastructure, and business entities were concentrated in six mega-cities. They banded together and, with an eye to the future, called the new country Westhem, claiming sovereignty over the Western Hemisphere. But that government only existed on paper and a few placeholder institutions.

The actual act of governing was outsourced to R1, a

conglomerate of businesses formed by absorbing all the other bankrupt corporations as they ceased to exist until it was the only corporation still producing, shipping and delivering goods.

R1 provided all the services you might ever need, filtered and piped all the water you would ever drink, and grew, harvested and processed all the food you would ever eat.

If you needed a job, R1 would hire you. The only requirement was to agree to abide by their Terms of Service. If you opted-out, you opted-out of civilization.

Over the next six years, R1 rebooted half of the world, recreating civilization in its own image, that being a corporate business with a well-defined hierarchy, a matrix management structure and quarterly profit goals.

The six mega-cities came under the explicit management of R1, with three divisions in charge of the entire Western Hemisphere and most of Oceania.

Stetson's parents were gone. His younger sister who had grown up, married, and started a family was gone. His own wife was gone.

Why he had carried on without them was a mystery he couldn't explain. Even with his training in forensics and investigation, his life defied logic.

And now, over twenty years since he first learned shorthand, with so much upheaval in between, Stetson Fox giggled at how ridiculous it was to indulge the thought of remembering how to write shorthand, and how stupid to read shorthand written by a kid who didn't seem to know how to write it.

It was a strange life in a strange world.

"Yep," his boss said. "I told you he'd be sitting around doing nothing."

Fox turned his chair around. His boss filled the doorway of his cubicle, but there was a man behind her, and he was much larger.

"What do you need?" Fox asked.

"This is Stanley Whitehead. You'll be reporting to him for a while."

Fox stood up, but it only improved the angle. The guy was huge. He didn't seem impressed with Fox, either.

"He's the best you got?" Stanley asked.

"No," she said. "He's familiar with the case, though. It's kind of a mess, to be honest."

"Fox, is it?" Stanley asked.

"Inspector Fox," he said.

"Take your day-to-day orders from Stanley," his boss said. "Until all the data updates, you're still reporting to me."

"I didn't know there was an opening in the organization," Fox said. "Maybe I would have applied."

"There wasn't," his boss said. "I'll be reporting to Stanley once the data updates, but he wants to get started on the Foster case."

"The Collective," Stanley said. "I'm here to deal with the Collective."

Fox nodded.

"I'll leave you two to it," his boss said.

Stanley had ordered a surveillance unit, and they parked down the street from the cafe in Old Town.

"Management rarely does field work," Fox said.

"I've got a lot to learn," Stanley said. "I figure I can learn on the job and I don't mind getting my hands dirty."

"Okay."

"Is there something you think I could have done better?"

Fox didn't want to anger his new boss within the first hour of meeting him, but he was coming to believe that it would be impossible not to piss this guy off. "Did you talk to someone about how to surveille a subject?"

"Of course. They said I needed a robo-van. Plug in the subject to the A.I., and get a list of hot spots, then tell the robo-van where to go. Here we are."

"This subject, Ashton Gray, is not like other opt-ins. His father is the Chief Minister. It's not as simple as asking the A.I. where to find him."

"I know that. I'm new, but I'm not an idiot."

"That's not what I meant."

"Well, how about you tell me what you meant, inspector?"

"Inspector?" Fox said, "I hardly know her."

"Is that supposed to be funny?"

"Nah. I'm just stalling."

"Get on with it."

Fox took a moment for an extra breath. "You're aware that the church has their own security service?"

"Everyone knows that."

"The church also has an arrangement with R1 changing the Terms of Service and the Opt-In agreement. The data privacy laws are applied differently to ordained ministers and members of staff of the church."

"So what?"

"So it means our own data inquiries limit the results of queries to the database. The A.I. is trained to comply. You need a special Decision Document, c-c'd to the church, to override the limits for detailed results. Even then, the A.I. is restricted from formatting the results."

"What does that mean?"

"If you got the detail, it would be a raw data dump. You'd have to build a results table by hand."

"Well, how the fuck do you do that?"

"A few of us know how."

Stanley stared at the monitors, each one showing a different drone feed of the streets surrounding the cafe. "So what are you saying? This is a waste of time."

It was, but Fox didn't dare say that. "I'm just trying to figure out what you want, and how to be of best service."

"I thought you were working this case already?"

"I'm tracking connections to Jaylend Foster. I hadn't investigated Ashton Gray as a subject."

"What were you waiting for?"

"Enough evidence to get the Decision Document signed, but I have seen nothing yet—"

"I know for a fact he's dealing drugs," Stanley said, turning away from the monitors to glare at Fox. "I have a witness that has seen him getting the drugs, taking the drugs, and distributing the drugs."

"What drug?"

"Candy."

"The kids' drug."

"It's still an illegal substance and a goddam violation of Terms of Service, I don't care if it's R1 or the church. You can't fucking do it."

Fox gave his new boss a moment to catch his breath. When Stanley looked back at the monitors, Fox asked, "Is the witness reliable?"

"It's my goddam daughter," he said. "Is that reliable enough for you?"

It wasn't but, again, Fox would not mention it.

They sat in silence for what seemed an eternity but, when

Fox checked his computer, was only twenty minutes.

"So this is what a stakeout is like?" Stanley asked.

"I guess."

"Haven't you been on one?"

"No."

"So what do you do?"

"There's a team that specializes. You plan out the observation points, identify all the contacts, and then you work out with the Surveillance Team and the A.I. to identify the best places to look. The team uses a mix of boots on the ground, eyeballs, and drones to cover the high-probability spots."

Stanley pondered this. "Why don't we just ask the A.I. for a location?"

"If it's an R1 opt-in, that's what you do. We don't surveille them."

"No?"

"No. You put in the query, mark the record for collection, then assign the task to Collections Team."

"Then why do we have a Surveillance Team?" Stanley asked.

"Because the opt-outs, here in Old Town, don't show up in the data. The farther you get from New Town, the fewer cameras there are. You put a bunch of boots on the ground, or park eyeballs in the neighborhoods, people avoid it."

"How do they know to avoid it?"

"Low-power amplitude modulation," Stetson said.

"What?"

"AM Radio, like the old days. It's like every block has their own station, and they let everybody know what's going on. You tune in with a crystal set, then tell all your friends over the fence in the back yard."

"I'll be damned."

Stanley took another moment to ponder. "What about drones?"

"They work great," Fox said, "but they get shot down."

"How the hell do they shoot them down?"

"Jam signals, electromagnetic pulse, or shoot them with a goddam gun if it stops long enough."

"They got guns?"

Fox nodded. There weren't a lot of them, but it was fun to see Stanley work this out in his head.

"They ever shoot us?"

"Not in a couple of years."

A few minutes later, Stanley tapped one of the monitors. "There he is. Just like the goddam A.I. predicted."

Ashton was walking alone, his visor down over his face, and lights flashing as he likely watched some programming. As he approached the cafe, he stopped and looked up, then his head turned toward their surveillance van.

"I think he sees us," Stanley said.

Ashton waved his fingers over his pocket computer and then seemed to talk into his visor.

"How do we listen to what he's saying?" Stanley asked.

"We can't. The church uses different encryption. I'm sure we can break it, but we don't. It's part of the agreement."

"That's stupid."

Ashton leaned against the side of the building, his visor dark now, most likely in pass-through mode.

"What's he doing?"

"Waiting."

"For what?"

"A ride."

A large robo-van arrived at high speed, dropping on

the street a few feet from Ashton, who hopped into it and lifted off as quickly as it arrived.

"Can we follow it?" Stanley asked.

"Yes, but I'll bet my life he's just going home."

"Why's that?"

"We can't follow him home. He lives in the church village, and we can't cross into that area unless accompanied by Church Safety personnel."

"Are you shitting me?"

"I shit you not. We can't get within five miles of his house."

"The stupid Terms of Service agreement?"

"Yes."

"Goddam son of a bitch."

# # # #

Marie Gray was in the kitchen with two of her house helpers, overseeing the dinner preparations, when their Safety Team helper came to the door.

"A robo-van is incoming. It's young Mr. Gray."

"Thank you," Marie said. She asked one of the helpers to prepare Ashton's favorite snack—peanut butter toast with cinnamon and sugar—and went to greet him.

"Is Dad home?" Ashton asked.

"He's at church."

"Cool." Ashton started up the stairs.

"Do you want some peanut butter toast?"

"Is it real peanuts?"

"Mm-hmm."

"Have them bring it to my room."

A few minutes later, as the helpers were ready to put the roast in the oven, the Safety Team helper informed her that another robo-van was incoming. "It's your husband."

Again, she went to the front door. "Is everything okay, Rohn?"

He seemed distracted and looked at the atrium like he'd never been there before. "Where's Ashton?"

"In his room, eating peanut butter toast."

Rohn went up the stairs without another word.

Marie started back to the kitchen, but it was unusual to have both arrive this early for supper.

Succumbing to the sin of curiosity, she went up the stairs. From there she saw a full Church Safety Team deployed out front, and another team arrive.

As she approached Ashton's room, Rohn stepped out with Ashton following him.

"What's going on?"

"Nothing," Ashton replied.

"It's not nothing," Rohn said.

Marie followed them into Rohn's home office.

"This doesn't concern you," Rohn said.

"If it's about my son, it concerns me."

"Fine."

"It's nothing," Ashton said.

Rohn stood next to his desk, staring down at Ashton seated on a chair. Marie sat on the sofa, out of the way.

"Here it is," Rohn said, waving his fingers over his pocket computer. "Pattern of behaviors consistent with trade in prohibited substances."

"That's bullshit," Ashton said. "They're idiots. Ignore them."

"It's serious, and we have to respond."

"Is it true?" Marie asked.

Rohn glanced at her. "Is it?"

"No. I'm not trading in prohibited substances."

"Are you taking drugs?"

"Everybody does."

"So that's yes."

"I have. Sure."

"For the love of God," Rohn said and sat down behind his desk with a great sigh.

"It's not a big deal," Ashton said.

Marie ventured a question: "What's going on?"

Rohn took a deep breath. "R1 Security submitted a formal request with the Safety Team to gain access to data concerning your son's movements, contacts and communications for the past seven months, citing trade in prohibited substances."

"Oh my."

"It's not a big deal, Mom."

"It is a big deal," Rohn said. "This sort of behavior can keep you from ever being a minister. And, I might add, it could keep you out of heaven."

"Heaven sounds boring."

Marie gasped.

"Marie, please."

"I'm sorry, but I can't believe what I'm hearing. It's like I don't even know who he is."

"Marie, we will handle this." Rohn leaned back in his chair and raised the pocket computer to his face. "Computer, gather all communications made by Ashton Rohn for the past six months."

"Wait," Ashton said. "You can do that?"

"Of course I can."

"But that was all private."

"It's listed in the Opt-in agreement."

"R1 does that stuff, but I didn't think we did."

"The Church Safety Team has access to all data. As head of the church, I also have access."

"That sucks."

Rohn waved his fingers over the computer and read

in silence for a minute.

"So you just broke up with Novalee?"

"Yeah. She was a pain."

"Wait, I thought you two were just friends," Marie said.

Ashton shrugged.

"Her father just joined R1 Security. I think he was pissed at not getting the VP Messaging position."

"The guy is a total wank."

"Ashton, please," Marie said. "Language."

"Sorry to tell you this, Mom, but not only am I a notorious drug dealer, but I also use the word 'wank.'"

"Don't be rude," she said.

"And it looks like you're now in a relationship with Karas Davidson?"

Ashton shrugged again.

"That's nice," Marie said. "I like her."

Rohn placed his hands on the desk. "Well, it seems your ex-girlfriend's father is out for vengeance."

"I told you it wasn't a big deal."

"Listen," Rohn said, standing up and moving to the side of his desk again. "It could be a big deal, but we can take care of this. First, you have to stop all use of Candy, and you sure as hell can't buy it, sell it or give it away. Nothing. Understand?"

Ashton nodded.

"Tell Karas to avoid Novalee for a while until we figure this out."

"Fine."

"Why were you at her house the other day?"

Ashton thought for a moment. "Oh, I was hoping I could get her sister to show me how to read shorthand, or whatever."

"Why would you want to know that?"

"I'm just trying to help a friend."

"Okay, well, don't involve yourself with that, or any kind of cursive writing, for a while. Got it?"

Ashton nodded.

Rohn turned to Marie. "So you'll see about supper?"

# # # #

Fox and Stanley had been in the surveillance robo-van for so long that they'd each relieved themselves twice using the lavatory in back, and had food delivered once. Fox knew things about his new boss that he'd never be able to forget. The sounds he made while eating were one thing, but he farted each time he urinated.

"How long do you want to wait?" Fox asked. They were parked on the street outside the main gate of the church village.

"As long as it takes."

"It could take two weeks to get a response."

Stanley scoffed. "I told Connor this was important. He brought me here to take care of this very thing."

"Yeah, but…"

"But what?"

"We don't know for sure the minister's son is working with the Collective. He might just be getting drugs for himself and some friends."

"Doesn't matter. It's a violation. The goddam church thinks it can do whatever it wants, and it's out of control."

Fox wanted to point out that the church could, in fact, do whatever it wanted. Besides the operating agreement with R1 granting the church autonomy, including its own armed security forces, the village they were prohibited from entering was surrounded by an eight-foot brick wall topped with iron spikes. There were lookouts every tenth of a mile stationed behind bullet proof glass, and church faithful, committed to keeping evil-doers on the outside, patrolled around the clock.

These church devotees had been God-fearing at some point, but now they feared everything outside of the church.

The walls were a mile long on each side, protecting a million people snug and secure within, forming a complete city within New Town. They had their own supply chain for raw materials. They built the shelter, delivered the food, purified the water and managed the waste. With their food production facility within, the church could withstand a siege of several years, to put it in medieval terms.

But Stanley thought his strongly worded email to his boss would somehow gain them entry.

While they waited, Fox had been expanding his search for data related to the case. Using a pivot table of his own design, he realized Stanley's daughter had been linked with Ashton.

Fox heaved a great sigh.

"You find anything?" Stanley asked. "You've been banging away at the thing long enough. Let me see."

Stanley grabbed the computer. "There's nothing here."

Fox suppressed a chuckle. He had set the computer to hide its display if he were not the one touching the control panel. "It's hard to get anywhere with the church. I mean, I've had no luck."

Stanley handed back the computer. "What do you suggest?"

"I think extended surveillance of the minister's entire family. We know they come out some time, if only for the services downtown. They got churches all over New

Town, and a few ministries in Old Town, right?"

"I guess."

"We keep pushing for the old data and gather as much as we can on our own of new data."

Stanley pondered this. "Maybe I'm not following."

"We review all that by hand and try to see the pattern, but also feed the A.I. and see what it gets."

"Huh. Okay."

"The A.I. is great for known associates. There are too many connections to traverse on our own."

"How long will that take?"

"A few months. Maybe a year."

"What?" Stanley lifted his bulk to turn in his seat. "I can't wait that long. I need something now."

"I don't know who told you otherwise, but these investigations take a long time."

Stanley chewed his lip, shook his head, looked at the ceiling. "What about the writing person?"

"The who?"

"The old woman who teaches them kids to write."

"What about her?"

"Let's bring her in, put pressure on her, and see what she knows."

Fox measured his words. "I've looked into her a bit, but I think she just teaches writing."

"Well, look some more, then bring her in."

"I guess—"

"No guessing, goddammit. You get me a report of her activities that makes it look like there's something there. Because I know there's something going on. She has access to these kids and fills their heads with that shit writing by hand nonsense."

"It's not nonsense."

"It's the dumbest shit ever. Not only does writing take

longer to do, you need paper and ink and all kinds of shit, and then nobody can read it. Dumbest goddam thing ever."

Then Stetson Fox understood. Abel Barker's shorthand notation wasn't like any standard notation on purpose. Abel created his own writing system to ensure his journal stayed personal.

The A.I. had never figured out even simple cursive writing because no one had bothered to teach it, and much of the written knowledge of the time before incorporation had been discarded by thick-skulled fools like Stanley who, given a semblance of power in R1, lacked foresight.

Jaylend was teaching her students to encrypt their journal entries in an unbreakable cipher.

Not completely unbreakable. Ham-fisted ignorami like Stanley would break the person to reveal the cipher. And there would be no putting those broken people back together again.

CHAPTER THIRTY-ONE

Leah sat in her room with Ilasha and wrote in her journal:

She's quieter now. They have her on Steady Jr., I'm pretty sure. She seems like a lot of kids her age, which means she's drugged.

I almost said it's for the best, but caught myself. It's weird how things pop in your head and if you don't question where they came from, you believe them.

'It's for the best' was a thing my dad wrote when he started in Messaging at work, and everybody loved it and thought he was a genius.

This was when Karas was just born, and things were still pretty weird after the fighting and the disasters and the incorporation. I guess people were still angry and distraught, and weren't so sure about the future.

'It's for the best' became like a catchphrase, and they used it on product advertising, and then the government managers would say it when talking about how the corporation was going to manage things, and then everybody started saying it.

We don't say it as much, but it shows up from time to time. No one ever talks about whether anything was for the best. My dad says it's because there are always bigger fish to fry, which is dumb because there aren't fish anymore except in an aquarium in New Minneapolis, or so I've been told.

My dad got a promotion because of that one stupid statement, and at least for him things were for the best. But not so much for everyone else.

I know there are places in Old Town where people have a hard time surviving. If they don't have solar on their roof, it gets hard to cook or pump water. If they don't even have a roof, then they're miserable all the time.

If they don't have access to the clean water, then they're either sick or dying.

They get angry at each other a lot, trying to figure out how to survive. Bad things happen in the dark, and they patrol the streets themselves to stop them. They could call in Cheney Security, but only if they opt into the service agreement.

And people in Old Town would rather die than opt into the service agreement.

I don't understand all the details, but I see how people live here, in New Town, with the service agreement. It doesn't seem perfect either.

My dad seems pretty happy, but he has a good job and doesn't have to wear the visor all the time. The people wearing visors don't seem like people at all. I can't tell if they're happy. They just seem to be there.

If that's what it's like to wear a visor, then maybe I understand why the people in Old Town are fine taking care of things themselves, as best they can.

I think maybe I'd like to—

"How's this?" Ilasha asked as she thrust her journal in front of Leah. She'd taken one of Leah's journals and was practicing her cursive. She'd started with Jaylend, too, same as Leah had ten years before, to learn to write.

She'd written:

Way up north, in a valley surrounded by mountains, is heaven, where everyone is happy and lives forever. There's clean water to drink and lots of nutritious food to eat, and they always project your favorite show.

I hope that's where my mommy and daddy went. I hope they are happy in heaven and are laughing a lot.

I want to go to heaven and live there forever with my family, especially my brother, who I miss a lot too.

"Can you read it?" Ilasha asked.

Leah nodded. Her throat had tightened up.

"Should I write some more?"

"Yes," Leah whispered.

"What should I write now?"

"Did your mother or father ever tell you stories?"

Ilasha nodded.

"Write down those."

Leah closed her eyes. She was going to write something else, too, but needed to think about this sadness she felt. Jaylend had taught her not to push away sadness or anger, but to think about them, and why they were visiting, and to think about what she could do about whatever it was that caused it.

If there was something she could do, she'd think about doing it. There was nothing to be done, and so she just had to practice breathing until she felt calm again.

The important thing was to not hide from those emotions. Also, you couldn't let them control you or they'd ruin your day. At least that's how Jaylend explained it.

The bedroom door swung open and Karas stepped in, closing the door behind her. "I need to talk to you."

"I'm busy."

Ilasha glanced up from her journal but kept writing.

Karas leaned close to Leah. "I need to use your room?"

"No. And why are you asking?"

"Ashton is coming over and we want some time alone."

"Ew, hell no."

"Come on," Karas said. "I'll get you something. You want some candy?"

"Of course not," Leah said. "You shouldn't either."

"I think he can get you a bunch of journals and pens."

This gave Leah pause, but she shook her head. "Why is

he even coming here?”

"It's part of his youth ministry," Karas said. "He's coming to visit with Ilasha."

Ilasha glanced up but returned to her journal, again.

"Use Dad's office," Leah said.

"Why are you being a bitch?"

Ilasha raised her head and studied them.

"You're upsetting Ilasha," Karas said.

"Wait," Leah said, stopping Karas from leaving. "Let me think about it."

CHAPTER THIRTY-TWO

Jaylend was at her desk in the front room when Blossom barked once from her perch on the chair by the window. The water truck was parked outside, and Carl, the delivery man, was gathering jugs.

Blossom barked twice more when there was a knock on the door.

Jaylend put away her journal, locked the desk, and hid the key in the parrot cage. Of course, anyone who intended trouble for her would not bother knocking. To lead a quiet life, one had to be vigilant and careful. You had to avoid paranoia, however, because the cost was too great.

"Hello Carl," she said, opening the door. "Am I short creds?"

"Sorry to bother you," he said, "but there's a message for you at the cafe. They said it was urgent."

"Who said it was urgent?"

Carl shrugged and lowered the lid on her delivery bin. "I don't know her name. I just deliver the water."

Jaylend buttoned up the house and took Blossom next door. The note could be a ruse by thieves to get her away.

This was the safest way to conduct herself, and no interruption, no matter how innocent, should be allowed to jeopardize her life.

Hardly a week went by without a burglary or robbery, sometimes even as the neighborhood watch passed by the house, thieves took what they could conceal on their body and then blended in with foot traffic.

The neighbors would watch for anything out of the ordinary, but they wouldn't risk their lives to intervene. Jaylend wouldn't want them to, anyway.

Her most valuable asset was the battery pack for the solar array, strong enough to run the house-water filter, but its bulk also made it the most difficult thing to steal. Still, it could happen, and a single stupid act could crush the tiny life she'd built.

Life had always been that way, of course, but now it all seemed so precarious...

Jaylend pushed the negative thoughts away as she walked, deciding to appreciate the sunshine. She'd make the most of the interruption by visiting the market to see if there were vegetables or fruit she might afford.

She happened upon a few birds, and noticing a nest, groaned with joy. That didn't happen every day.

The cafe served as a de facto postal exchange, with people leaving notes for each other, and word being sent out, or not, as the various delivery people stopped by.

"I was told there's a message for me," she said.

Finally, he understood. "Oh, hang on."

He leaned his head into the office doorway and a few moments later Suja, the proprietor, stepped out.

"One of your students," Suja said as she offered the envelope.

"She seem stressed?"

Suja shook her head. "Seemed happy. Took some tea and a cake with her."

Jaylend glanced to either side of the cafe. "Nothing else unusual."

"A few kids from New Town, mostly regulars. A few opt-ins that seemed curious. A couple of fresh faces, but nothing suspicious."

"Thanks."

Jaylend recognized the handwriting on the envelope: it was from Leah. She ordered tea and took a seat by the window before opening it.

Outside, a few carts selling household utensils lined the street, heading into Old Town. An electric van, laden with furniture strapped to the roof, rolled along the road. At the far corner, two Security guards walked toward New Town.

Things were normal.

She opened the note and read: "I'd like to see you for a supplemental lesson. I'll be here at three o'clock. Hope to see you."

It was signed, but Jaylend didn't need the signature to know it was from Leah.

She left the envelope at the cafe and took the note, along with a scone, down the street to the bench.

It was a warm afternoon, but the shade made it pleasant. The sky was clear, and she noticed cargo planes descending toward the landing strip, which didn't happen often.

Across the street, a man caught her eye. It was Inspector Fox, dressed like an Old Town pedestrian. He strolled to the corner, crossed, and approached her bench.

"May I join you?" he asked.

"Questions for me?" Jaylend asked.

Sitting on the far end of the bench, he reached in his pocked and removed a gadget. It was a lighter, which he snapped open and sparked. "For that note."

Jaylend dipped the corner in the flame and let it burn a few seconds before dropping it on the brick beneath the bench.

Once the note was consumed, Stetson Fox ground the ash under his boot.

"Who said chivalry is dead?" Jaylend said.

"I used to use shorthand myself," he said. "Long, long time ago."

"You mentioned," Jaylend said. Then, so as not to offend, asked, "What system?"

"Greg, I guess."

Jaylend smiled. "If only you hadn't opted-in, I might still teach you."

"I'm too old for that."

He seemed to mean it. "So why are you here? Scare tactic?"

He paused. "We'll be talking to all of your students."

"Why?"

"Patterns of conspiracy." He whispered so low, she wasn't sure she understood him. Her heart pounded, alert to a danger in his voice.

"Patterns? Is this because of that stupid artificial intelligence?"

Fox shook his head. "Something even stupider than that: my boss."

Jaylend almost laughed, but her heart was still racing. "I teach children the dying art of cursive writing."

"Someone stupid might interpret it as encryption and deception."

"Of for fuck's sake," she said. She was too disturbed to care about being rude.

"Why are you telling me this," she whispered.

"In case there's something you can do."

"It's not like I can leave," she said. "I have nowhere else to go."

"Can you hide?" Stetson asked. "For a few days at

least? He's not patient enough to sustain an investigation. Or he'll do something stupid and get himself banished."

"It's not a simple thing," Jaylend said. "Trust is earned down here. Betrayals happen too often."

She looked up again at the tree and was relieved to see a robin with a worm in its beak, likely on its way to feed its hatchlings.

"I'll stall them as long as I can," he said. "But my boss will act. He's bucking for a promotion or has a grudge to settle."

Jaylend stared, offering nothing but her silence.

"I'm sorry I can't do more."

"Thanks for the warning," she said. "If it is a warning."

CHAPTER THIRTY-THREE

When Jaylend returned to the cafe, she took the long way around, going first to the market, then the town square, and walking a full mile in a wide loop to reveal anyone following her. She knew they could just watch the cafe around the clock and see her, but this meandering return calmed her, as if the conscious act would help defend herself and Leah.

Inspector Fox had made it clear that they were watching her, and every action from that point forward was suspect. Even passing a note back at this point would be tantamount to conspiring to conceal from the corporation, and would be deemed an act against the state, encrypted or not.

Passing notes had gotten her into trouble forty-five years before, in fifth grade, and it would get her in trouble again.

Of course, instead of a trip to the principal's office for a lecture about paying attention, now there would be an armed escort to an interrogation room where they would torture her.

Or so she'd been told.

No. There was no reason to think that. Worry about the future was the only torture, and it was all her own fault. She'd already lived through terrible things.

It was okay to be afraid. Fear was a part of modern living. You had to channel it into action.

Jaylend arrived at the cafe, ordered her tea and took a table away from the window, in the corner opposite her normal seat.

When Leah arrived, Jaylend knocked on the manager's office open door. "Can I use the conference room?"

Suja pointed to the key hanging on the wall. "You'll go if they come for you?"

Jaylend nodded. "I'm not hiding."

"Is this room secure?" Leah asked.

Jaylend looked around. The walls were water stained and cracked. The ceiling was a patchwork of metal sheeting attached to whatever held up the roof. An ancient table of pressed wood, its corners warped and coming apart, stood in the center. She and Leah sat on folding metal chairs. "This room is as secure as things get in Old Town, which is more secure than things in New Town."

Leah took a breath. "I have to get there. I have to leave New Town."

Jaylend wasn't expecting this. "Where would you go?"

"To the unincorporated area, with her brother. Abel and I have decided."

"You have?"

"We've talked," Leah said. "We're in agreement, and we're taking Ilasha with us."

"Okay."

"But we need your help."

"Okay, I just don't know what to do."

"Can you try?"

"It's a terrible time." Jaylend explained the visit from

Inspector Fox. "I don't know if he's trying to warn me, or if he's set a trap."

"But people try to leave, don't they?"

"People try, yes. When they've lost all other hope."

Leah looked around, as if there might be answers somewhere in the room. "I don't want to live here anymore, and I don't think Ilasha or Abel want to either."

Jaylend shook her head. "You would need a corporate executive, someone very high up, like your father, to arrange such things. To provide transport, approve requests, and do it all under the scrutiny of the A.I. and security. I'm not even sure he could pull it off."

They were silent, and Jaylend believed Leah saw the impossibility of things.

"Could we hide in Old Town?"

"For a short while."

Leah panted as she stared at the table, her eyes dilated.

"Are you okay?"

"Of course not."

"I mean, are you going to vomit?"

Leah nodded.

Jaylend found a waste basket in the corner and held it as Leah vomited. She accepted the water Jaylend offered and sat back in the chair.

"We're trapped?"

Jaylend believed they were, but didn't dare say. Instead, she said, "We have to stay strong, and carry the light forward for others."

"What light?" Leah asked.

"Hope."

Leah nodded. "How do we do that? What's the point of hope when you're trapped and have no hope?"

"We can't see the path right now, but I know it's

there."

"So you can't see the light either."

This was a critical moment. Jaylend had hoped she would be of use some day, when the opportunity presented itself, but now there was only this one problem. If she could not do anything for Ilasha and Abel, Leah would lose hope.

"Do you still have all of your journals?" Jaylend asked.

Leah shook her head.

"Who took them?" Jaylend asked, the tension in your throat raising her voice and surprising herself.

"No one," Leah said. "I shredded them all the past two days."

"Page by page?"

"Page by page."

"That's good," Jaylend said. "How did you know to do it?"

"The minister's son and my sister started using my room, and I didn't want to leave my journals there."

Jaylend nodded. "Keep this with you," Jaylend said as she offered Leah a pocket-sized notebook. "And only practice your script."

Leah rubbed the notebook between her hands and flipped through the pages, rubbing a page between her fingers. Jaylend was pleased, if only for that moment, that Leah appreciated the beauty of a blank notebook.

"Thank you," Leah said. "I've been helping Ilasha. She enjoys practicing. I think it's the only thing she enjoys, right now."

"You're giving her hope."

"I'd like to give her family, and a place to live."

Jaylend nodded again.

Leah slumped in her seat. She seemed exhausted, but at least she didn't look as sick as before. "What's it like in the herd?" Leah asked. "I mean, Family Valley, assuming that's where her parents went, what would it be like to live in the herd?"

"Some of it is bleak, but not all of it. I heard they live in the abandoned homes from before, in the cities and suburbs of what used to be."

"Like Old Town?"

"Yes, a lot like that. They spend much of each day getting water and food to live, and they all work together to make the best of things."

"But they can't leave?"

"The wranglers see to that."

Leah sat up in her chair, a glimmer in her eyes. "The families have each other. That's how they survive."

Jaylend nodded. "It's the way it always has been, I suppose."

Leah thought a moment, her eyes narrowed and her lips moving, as if she were chewing it over.

# # # #

Leah exited the train, plodding through the crowd as the visored passengers marched past her, their steps directed by the A.I. to avoid collisions but leaving no room for Leah to walk. She didn't care how slow her progress.

Her mind struggled with how to get Ilasha out of New Town without alerting security. They'd chipped her clothing, and her face was likely on a high priority tracking; even if she could get Ilasha out of her chipped clothing, it was possible they'd implanted a chip under Ilasha's skin. How would she ever figure out that problem?

Even if she could solve all that, she still had to distract her family enough to somehow get Ilasha to Old Town without drawing the attention of security guards patrolling the city.

When at last she was on the sidewalk and the crowds thinned out, she noticed someone walking beside her.

"I know where you've been," Novalee, the girl next door, said. She removed her visor and stood in Leah's way.

"What?"

"You were at the cafe in Old Town, talking to that witch."

"She's not a witch. And I haven't opted-in, so it doesn't matter, anyway. I can talk to anyone I want."

Novalee smirked. "That's not true."

"Okay, fine," Leah said, and stepped past her.

Novalee walked with her. "I'd like you to do something for me."

"What? No."

"It's for your own good."

"Please leave me alone."

"You don't want to lose little what's-her-name, do you?"

Leah stopped walking. "She's had enough trouble."

"If you help me, nothing would have to happen to her. You could go on being the big sister she never had."

Leah walked on. She'd never liked Novalee before and now was repulsed and nauseated. Listening to her talk was making Leah's legs wobble. She worried she might stumble.

"I don't like your big sister, and I know you don't either. She and Ashton had sex, I'm guessing. All you have to do is tell my dad, and she can go away."

"No. That's insane."

"They violated their terms of service. Nothing bad will happen, you know. Just a few weeks of rehabilitation. That will give you some quality alone time with Ishkabibble."

"Leave me alone."

"Karas doesn't care about the little kid. Not like you do. She just uses her to get Ashton's attention."

They were at the door of their building. Leah said nothing else, afraid she'd vomit.

"Think about it. No one would have to know it was you." Novalee stayed close behind her. "I would do it myself, but my dad thinks it'd look bad if I was the witness. Can I count on you?"

Leah shook her head and went up the elevator, averting her eyes from Novalee until they were on their floor. In the reflection of the stainless steel doors, Leah noticed Novalee decorated her R1-issued uniform with a sash, and had painted a geometric design on her visor with nail polish.

"Leave us alone," Leah said, her voice rasping and weak. She hurried to her apartment without looking back.

# # # #

Leah rode to the last stop at the end of one of the earlier shifts and then lingered on the street. She wore a visor to blend in, but kept it in pass-through mode.

Visored heads strolled past, hundreds of people a minute discharged from the train as the hundreds waiting to board pushed past them in the opposite direction, two masses of bodies roiling past each other like one of those simulations of two galaxies colliding, the gravity pulling the stars into a new, third shape. As with the galaxies, there were only a few collisions, as the visors warned their host of impending collision and directed next steps to protect their host, doing this in coordination with the other visor.

No one ever became angry at the detours or the odd jostle, as they were entertained by whatever was projected. If they missed a train, they stood and waited for the next one, no worse off than if they'd made it.

In the morning, Leah got Ilasha ready and took her to school. Then she made her way to the train station on the line Abel would take.

Clutched in her hand was a note she prepared that morning, torn out of the small notebook Jaylend had given her, and folded into a square the size of her thumbnail.

She watched as the train arrived and saw Abel's black hair, and made her way to that car. She donned her visor and boarded the train.

Abel offered her his seat. As they switched, she slipped the note into his hand.

In the evening, she was on the train before Abel boarded and kept her visor off. As he walked past, he dropped the note in her visor as she raised it to put on her head.

They didn't speak and didn't look at each other.

When Leah read that note, clutched in her hands as she sat in her bed, huddled beneath the covers, she realized she loved this boy.

She thought about what she would say in her next note, how she might suggest to him she would help him with Ilasha without suggesting too much. Could she suggest too much about anything, though, having suggested he violate his terms of service and kidnap his own sister?

He needed to understand that she wasn't scolding him, but trying her best to help. That she wanted to make things right, but couldn't undo what had happened.

She wanted him to know that she admired and liked him. She would do whatever she could to help him.

Leah paused and stared at the ceiling.

She loved him, and would die for him because nothing else mattered in this world.

CHAPTER THIRTY-FOUR

Abel was almost grateful for the challenge of his intractable problem. Having something to mull over helped pass the time working in fulfillment.

Sensors tracked his every move, logged the data to servers, and artificial intelligence reviewed the data, meaning he could not escape this place without detection.

In pursuit of his baccalaureate, he had studied the various technologies needed to track people. He knew full well the problem he faced: how to avoid the corporation's ability to track his every movement.

In his academic studies, these were presented as challenges overcome by the corporation which allowed for greater freedoms for those opted-in, as the solutions provided stability, growth and happiness for society.

One of his instructors joked about tracking, logging and interpreting data as the Holy Trinity, and two days later they got a new instructor and nobody made jokes after that.

Over the years, Abel overheard his father discussing the Holy Trinity technologies. He told anecdotes or vented frustrations with no specifics, but Abel had connected the pieces, filling in the gaps between what he learned in academic studies and his father's vague remarks.

The first problem, defeating the tracking, was the most important. Every article of clothing he wore had chips embedded that could be tracked at great distances by the sensors installed all across the city. Each doorway and lamp post had a sensor. Any spot in the city without a doorway or a nearby lamp post had a tower installed with more sensors.

The corporation had blanketed the city with sensors.

Besides the sensors tracking embedded chips, there were cameras mounted in even greater numbers, and those cameras moved, zoomed and focused to capture the faces of passers-by. If chips didn't track you, the cameras would. Also, a mismatch between the face and the clothing's unique ID was noted.

Microphones picked up everything said aloud. They listened on trains and buses, on the streets and in the buildings. The microphones even listened inside of private homes.

This problem was well known to every incorporated citizen, as they taught their children, that complaining could kill their family. Children played games about the monster who listened to their every word. They collapsed from anxiety attacks and shivered with night terrors about the monster waiting to take them away if they said the wrong thing.

The corporation's A.I. ignored much of this, it seemed, because no family had been destroyed because of incidents with children. Neither did the corporation attempt to dispel the myth, as it seemed to enhance their desired results.

Abel understood that each voice was unique. The A.I. could process the discussions, transcribing the words and searching for anything that indicated a conspiracy.

The device Leah had given him would hide their

voices. He still had to solve the problem of facial recognition and chipped clothing.

One day at the warehouse, during their break, as his coworkers sat still, transfixed by the stories projected on their visors, Abel noticed a worker enter the break area carrying his visor, rather than wearing it.

His face seemed familiar.

Before the man left, he glanced around and nodded at Abel. A moment later, Abel remembered how he knew him.

"John?" Abel said, catching up to him. "We were in Academics together."

"Oh, hey," John said. He studied Abel's face. "Barker, right?"

"Yes!"

John laughed. He seemed about to say something but laughed again, instead.

"I'm so glad I amuse you."

John cut his laughter short, wiped his eyes and took a breath. "Sorry, but you were supposed to be in charge of this place someday."

Abel stared.

"Your dad was the second most powerful man in the world."

"I'm aware."

"You were guaranteed a place in heaven but, instead, here you are."

"Here I am."

"I don't know if anyone has said this to you," John said, "but welcome to Fulfillment."

The next day, John approached Abel during break. "Sorry about yesterday," he said. "I asked around and heard about your family and everything."

"That's fine," Abel said. "I'm glad you enjoyed my pain and suffering."

"Okay. I said I was sorry."

Abel shrugged. "Of course. How stupid of me."

John was a little shorter than Abel with a slighter build. His uniform seemed intentionally loose, rather than sloppy. He had wide-set, prominent eyes and a large smile. Dark hair framed his face. He took a small tin box from his pocket and flipped a switch on the side. "Let me make it up to you."

"Is that what I think it is?"

John nodded. "Can't be too careful."

Robots, followed by workers, moved products by the pallet, crisscrossing the floor from stack to stack. As Abel shifted on his feet, John broke the silence.

"I thought you'd be in charge some day."

"Instead, I'm here."

John laughed, but not as hard as the day before. "I always figured I'd end up here. Like my old man spent all of his creds to get me into that school, but..." John waved his hand, pointing out the obvious.

With a quick smile, he said, "I can get you candy, marijuana, heroine... anything you want."

"What?"

"It can be a good time here in Fulfillment if you're willing to bend the rules."

"Okay."

"You good then?"

"I don't know," Abel said. "I'm not sure about anything."

"Sure," John said, "That's cool. Catch me later."

# # # #

It had taken Abel all of twenty minutes to learn everything he'd ever need to know to about working in Fulfillment: if he wasn't present at the start of his shift, he was docked an hour of credits plus time missed; if he was late from break, he was docked an hour of credits; and if he left before his shift was over, he was docked two hours of credits plus time missed.

The work involved following a robot around the distribution center as it retrieved items to be shipped. The desired item's name, quantity and identification number was listed on a screen. When the item was pulled from the shelf, that selected item's information displayed next to the desired item. Abel confirmed it had selected the correct product.

The robot's hydraulic limbs reached to the highest shelf as easily as the lowest. Even if the item wasn't there on the shelf, the robot handled the situation.

Clearly, this was busy-work to give humans something to do, rather than sit inside their assigned apartments day in, day out. They worked for their creds, but they didn't work hard.

The only challenge was not going berserk from the boredom.

# # # #

"How do you do it?" Abel asked. "How do you deal with this job every day knowing there's no chance of it ever changing?"

With a quick smile, John said, "I can get you candy, marijuana, heroine... anything you want."

Abel's robot beeped twice, getting his attention. "I'm coming."

John winked as he flashed the sound-canceling device in his palm. "Let me know."

# # # #

The next day, Abel waited for John to turn on his sound-canceling device. "I need to go somewhere without being tracked," Abel said.

John clicked his tongue. "You sure you just don't want some heroine?"

"I need to get to Old Town without the company knowing I went there."

John thought a moment, then made the clicking noise again. "You taking something, bringing something back, or just meeting someone."

"All of it, and I want to stay there."

John clicked his tongue several times in a row. "Find me tomorrow. That ain't easy."

"Thanks."

The next day, they met during Abel's break.

"When do you want to disappear?"

"Pretty soon."

"What do you want to take with you?"

"My little sister."

John nodded. "I was afraid you were going to say that."

"Can it happen?"

John laughed. "I can't do that."

"Do you know someone who can?"

"We got a good thing here," John said. "You'll get used to it."

"Then get me enough heroine to kill myself."

"Whoa. That went dark."

"It's been dark for me ever since…"

"I'll talk to some people."

"Thanks."

"Don't get your hopes up. If they pull too many strings at once, the A.I. gets its circuits in a knot, and then the techs come in and tear this place apart. Nobody wants that."

# # # #

A week later, John told Abel that it could happen. "They'll kill you if you screw up. The good news is it happens quickly. The bad news is you're dead and never going to heaven."

"Seems like a bargain."

John approached Abel a few days later and instructed him to purchase a new projector from R1.

"Why am I ordering from R1?"

"The obstacle is the way, buddy."

"I don't even use the projector I have."

"Well, you better start, buddy, because the system has to think you're someone who has gotten used to living within the Terms of Service."

The day after that, John told him to order a new visor. "And start wearing it. Your bare head sticks out like a sore thumb."

Then it was shoes, underwear, furniture and bed. He requested teeth cleaners, ultrasound shower attachment and yet another projector.

"You'd be amazed, buddy, how often people upgrade their projector," John explained. "It's like the idiots forget they ordered the previous one."

Each time they met, John explained a little more about

how the plan would work. It relied on the lag in data collection, data reporting, and interpreting of the results. "We're just using the system," John said. "Some day they'll fix it. Until then, this is the best option. It works if you're just a bit lucky."

"I don't feel lucky," Abel said.

"Then you need to start feeling differently."

The second replacement projector arrived. Abel opened the package and discovered that they stuffed the box with old cash, still the de facto currency for Old Town. It was time to go.

Abel and Leah met at church one last time. Abel had shared with Leah instructions on how to slip out of the city. They now had a rendezvous in Old Town with someone would move them to the next destination.

This element of mystery seemed dangerous, but they agreed it was not riskier than waiting for the corporation to decide their fate for them.

As their hands touched and they wrote in each other's palm, Leah's hands trembled with the realization it was time to go.

"Do you still want to?" he asked.

"Yes," she replied. "I'm sick of it all, and I don't want to die in this place."

They confirmed he would leave things for her at the train station near Ilasha's school, but that it wouldn't raise an alert because he'd be off the grid already at that point, and Leah would have abandoned her pocket computer and microwaved Ilasha's change of clothes.

"Are you scared?" he asked.

"Yes, but it doesn't matter," she replied. "I love you."

"I love you too."

John hinted that, when they made their move, a series of false positives planted in the system would distract the A.I. This, combined with the fact that the A.I.'s processing lagged two or more days behind actual events, would buy them enough cover.

The system devoted its priority processing to actively tracked individuals—opt-ins with a history of violation and a suspicious or escalating pattern of activity. The A.I. processed all the other tracking, facial and voice recognition, and interactions on the street when demands on the system subsided. It assigned anything warranting investigation to teams who reviewed, assembled and reported on those flagged events.

This led to another set of reviews, and additional use of A.I. to identify a round of investigations. All those secondary reviews could buy you a week or more of invisibility.

But you had to stay off the active tracking list. Those poor bastards, as John explained, couldn't fart on a train without Security following them the rest of the way home, sniffing their ass for further evidence of violating the Terms of Service.

Now, making last preparations, Abel brought two complete outfits into the kitchen and microwaved each article of clothing for twenty seconds. This, according to John, was long enough to short circuit the chips embedded in the clothes.

The visor was the toughest part, but he took it inside the bathroom where the sound of the ventilation fan and the waste trap operating would obscure the sounds made, allowing him to work without triggering an A.I. early warning.

With John, he had pilfered various tools from work, making sure they had neutralized the embedded chip on each tool.

Abel disassembled the visor and removed all the electronic components, dumping them in his shower. The biggest concern was that there might be a chip embedded in the plastic helmet. Once he gutted the various components, he found a sticker that was flush on the inside of the helmet, and the sticker itself was the chip.

With his outfit ready, he reconfigured the visor to cover more of his nose. He also stuck pieces of paper on his cheek and neck, confident it would confuse the facial recognition. (He also reminded himself to switch those pieces of paper around as he walked across the city, denying the A.I. the ability to build his fresh look as a profile to be tracked.)

When he set out, he was wearing three outfits in layers. Against his skin was vintage clothing to blend in with people in Old Town. On top of that was the R1-approved work uniform with neutralized tracking chips. On the outside he wore a new uniform, a size larger than normal, to fit over the other clothing.

He carried with him the outfits for Ilasha and Leah, tools and a few necessities.

With bland food in his belly and three layers of clothes on his back, Abel walked toward the train station. By his calculation, Leah would be setting out to pick up Ilasha from school. With a little luck, they'd meet in about two hours.

CHAPTER THIRTY-FIVE

At station number seven, Abel, surrounded by several dozen people, waited for the next train. It arrived with a blast of air and a chorus of visor alerts chiming in the crowd. Abel turned and went into the toilet room.

In the second stall, he removed his top layer of clothing, jamming it behind the waste trap. Then he waited for someone else to enter the toilet room.

His clothing now untraceable, Abel slipped outside when the door opened and a man wearing a visor stepped inside. If the A.I. did not flag his movement through the door, his last known presence would be in the second stall of the toilet trap at train station number seven.

Abel fell into step with the crowd leaving the station. He paid attention to the street signs because the route was committed to memory. Not wanting to provide the A.I. any previous histories to use in its analysis, this was his first time traveling the route.

He walked along a busy street with shops and diners. Now he needed the crowd to provide cover, using the overload of data gathering to delay detection by the A.I.

In the center of the shops was a toilet area and he went into the third stall. There he left the outfits for Leah and Ilasha hanging on the door hook. Then he removed his outer uniform, revealing the Old Town clothes underneath.

There was a risk that the clothing left behind would be found and turned in, but most people would wear a visor and wouldn't notice the clothing.

Back on the sidewalk, he looked around, wrestling with the urge to wait for them and help them with the remaining journey. John had said he'd need a little luck, but it felt now like they needed a lot.

But he had to stick to their plan for any of it to work. He turned and walked away, not wanting the A.I. to flag his presence or for a security patrol to challenge him.

# # # #

When the school day ended, Leah's tension eased as Ilasha hugged her in the waiting room.

"Are you tired?" Leah asked.

Ilasha shrugged. "No."

"Good, because we have to run an errand on the way home."

Ilasha shrugged once more.

They made their way to station number seven.

Leah held Ilasha's hand as they exited the toilet room. Dressed now in the Old Town clothes left in the stall by Abel, she felt conspicuous and vulnerable.

She also carried the shopping bag laden with the few purchases they'd made before changing clothes. She had purchased items they'd need the next couple of days. Of course she'd like to have purchased more, but that might have also set off an alert.

There were others like them, people dressed in Old Town style clothes and carrying purchases. It was a reasonable plan to slip away from New Town.

Still, they wouldn't blend in with the crowds, and Leah was more worried about the surveillance cameras and the A.I. than the visored people walking along the street. Ilasha seemed fine with the changes and the walking, so Leah set a brisk pace and kept moving.

Glancing at the people moving towards them, their faces almost obscured by visors, she thought about Abel's eyes, brown with flecks of gold. And he had long, black eyelashes.

At the edge of the shopping district, Leah wasn't sure which way to turn. She hadn't ever taken this path, which was one strategy she and Abel decided upon to foil the A.I., so she'd memorized the directions.

Not wanting to draw attention to themselves by standing still, she made a loop crossing streets, checking the street names. Feeling uneasy, as if being pursued, she turned right at the next corner.

"Here we go," she said.

"Okay," Ilasha answered.

The road took them away from the raised train line, and there were fewer pedestrians. It grew quieter. No one was outside the apartments at that moment, but she thought she heard something, so Leah made a cursory glance behind her.

A young woman walked towards them. She wore a recent R1 uniform, accessorized with a flower-pattern sash and a visor with a geometric design done in pastels. The young woman paused before continuing towards them.

Leah continued on but looked back; again the young woman paused. Something about her movements seemed familiar. Then she realized that the sash and geometric design on the visor were things Novalee did.

Leah felt vulnerable, as if she'd been caught outright.

"What are you doing?" Novalee asked, rushing up from behind. "Ilasha, are you okay?"

Novalee reached for her hand, but Leah put her body between them. "Leave us alone."

Novalee smiled. "All you had to do was say two words to my father about Karas, and I never would have bothered you again."

"Stop following us," Leah said, and backed away from Novalee, pulling Ilasha along by the hand.

"Fine by me," Novalee said. Then she took out her pocket computer and snapped a finger to place a call.

CHAPTER THIRTY-SIX

Ballard left the office a little early to nap before he had to change clothes for the evening. He and Tyra were going to a mid-week church service because her favorite band was playing. Ballard was more interested in the group opening for them, a cover band that played songs from before incorporation.

Young people didn't care about either band, so Karas and Leah were staying home with Ilasha, and he and Tyra would have the suite at church to themselves.

He took a robo-van to the roof of their apartment building and rode the elevator down a floor.

Ballard sang a song the band would play later that night, then stopped himself cold. He'd forgotten about the cameras and microphones, and he didn't want such recordings as part of his permanent record.

Of course, if none of the other things had happened, beginning with their adoption of Ilasha, his permanent record would be an electronic file with just his vital information listed.

Instead, there was a nightly query gathering up all sightings, recordings and tracking chip hits the system recorded. Every morning, a technician in one of the older buildings, stuck in a cubicle with stained carpeting under foot and ceiling tiles warped by a leaking roof, would review all the records in the query result set and place positives in his file.

Then, a more skilled analyst could piece together his movements and comments, mapping them to interpretations of his facial expressions. The result would be a timeline of his movements and encounters of the entire day, with reference links to everyone he met, and transcripts of what they said.

If what he heard was true, they would log his trips to the toilet, and include a chart in his file showing the tendencies, and raise an alert if you peed or pooped more than was predicted.

It was rare that anyone got in trouble for their toilet tendencies unless they said something treasonous while sitting on the can.

The risk was that those movements and comments could convince a Human Resources analyst that there might be a problem, and an investigation would ensue.

Once an investigation opened, your career was over.

Even if they found nothing, it would be enough to keep you from a promotion.

The reason for all this, of course, was to solve crimes. The effect was to suppress all individual expression of hate, anger or love. No one made jokes about anything that the corporation, the church, or the security forces did.

A joke like that might end your career.

A funny joke might end your life.

People in New Town didn't gather in cafes to talk or listen to music. They didn't go to concerts or sporting events. All that they did was work during their shift, go to church service once or twice a week, and stay in their apartment watching corporate-approved shows projected on walls. In between, they wore visors to continue watching the shows.

It was much safer to put on your visor and pretend like nothing else was happening. Maybe he should have done that, and turned his back on this new world, when Viktoria approached him about having a child from her egg and his sperm, and using Tyra as a surrogate.

As Ballard entered the hallway, he realized it was too quiet. The doors were thin, and he could hear what was being projected by his family inside.

Of course he was being paranoid. Just in case there was truth behind it, Ballard queued up the program to wipe their computers clean.

As he approached his apartment door, it swung open and Stanley Whitehead stood in the doorway, barring his entry. Behind him, Tyra and Karas sat on the floor. Behind them stood two security guards.

Stanley lunged at him, grabbing the computer from Ballard's hand. Ballard didn't flinch. Once his thumb pulled away from the screen, it began deleting data and would reset each machine within seconds. It might save them or it might not; it would be enough if it just annoyed or embarrassed Stanley.

"I'll need you to step back and sit on the floor," Stanley said.

Two security officers stepped out of apartments at one end of the floor, and two more security officers stepped out of apartments at the other end.

Ballard kneeled down and sat on his heels. He worried about what might have happened to Leah and Ilasha, but he didn't dare allow his face to betray what he was thinking.

CHAPTER THIRTY-SEVEN

Blossom barked a half dozen times, and Jaylend's heart beat with worry. A black van was parked on the street. First she checked that the windows and doors were locked. Then she returned to her study and closed its doors.

She sat at her desk with Blossom on her lap and drank the last of her tea. It was still at a pleasant temperature, and she needed to enjoy that moment.

Tea reminded Jaylend of her maternal grandmother, Caroline, who had lived alone for all the years Jaylend knew her.

Whenever they visited, Caroline had put on tea, offered cookies or cake, insisting on sitting to enjoy the tea when the temperature was right.

"If you can't enjoy a moment as simple and nice as this," Caroline would say, "you'll never find happiness in this world."

Once the tea had been drunk, she was fine with all interruptions, but not one second before.

Rather than put away the cup and saucer, Jaylend held Blossom close to her bosom and walked around the room.

She'd be happy, she reminded herself, if all she did for

the next twenty years was re-read these books. She'd be grateful for every second spent reading.

The hutch was laden with journals. Again, if she spent the next twenty years writing in a journal, she'd be happy and grateful about that, too.

Scattered on the shelves, cabinets and tables in the rest of the study were cards, notes and knickknacks gathered over a lifetime: presents given to her by her mother and grandmother, mementos taken from her father, aunts and uncles and grandparents, things that made no sense unless you held them and thought about them a moment to remind yourself where they came from, and who was it that made you want that thing.

The house itself had been Caroline's, who deeded it to Jaylend in a quit-claim when things turned sour. Caroline might have given it to one of Jaylend's cousins, but they all had scattered across the country and there wasn't much time to sort things out.

It all seemed a miracle to Jaylend that she had survived this long as her own person, refusing to opt-in, and making a life among people who were more interested in community than personal satisfaction.

It hadn't been an awful life, and was a very good one judging by several measures, such as being present and thoughtful with yourself and those in your life, despite living under a tyrannical regime and surrounded by mindless assholes staggering through life.

She had no regrets.

The black van was still the only thing out of the ordinary on the street, until two drones zipped past above the house. Her stomach tightened, and she had to force herself to swallow. It was her time.

Of course, she said this to herself ten times a week, but it had to be true one of these days.

Although she had never witnessed someone being taken away, she'd heard about it from neighbors or at the cafe. When they come for you, you never return. The ACLU will file a claim with R1, but it never results in the happy return of whomever they took.

Jaylend removed her copy of Don Quixote from the bottom shelf. It was her favorite novel, and she held it the way a child might hold a security blanket. The writer, Cervantes, had suffered imprisonment and slavery, but always kept the story he wanted to tell on his mind. Or maybe he didn't think of that story all the time, and just fought for his life, regardless.

She sat at her desk and picked out a new journal for her stack. She had several right there, and several more squirreled away in various places in the house. Her own mother had a thing for candles and stones, which were placed throughout the house because she believed they had healing powers and eased tension in the space. Jaylend thought the same thing about blank journals.

She grabbed two pens she liked and ink refills. She felt blessed to have lived so much of her life surrounded by books, and with the privilege to write on smooth paper with pens she loved and ink that would not wash away.

As she stood up, three security vans, marked and moving fast, screeched to a halt in front of the house. Blossom barked and squirmed to get free, but Jaylend held on. She'd be willing to drop the book and the journal, but not Blossom.

Jaylend hurried to the front door. She gave Blossom one more squeeze and then opened the door.

Two security officers in tactical gear grabbed her arms, and she screamed as Blossom hit the floor and cried out. Five more security officers ran inside and scattered into the house.

As the men secured her hands behind her back, Inspector Fox came to the door. He held Blossom in his arms.

"She's fine," he said.

Jaylend sobbed as it took her several seconds to catch her breath.

"Inspector Fox," she said at last. "What a surprise."

"Sorry about all this," Inspector Fox said. "We like to be sure about things so that no one gets hurt. I promise you it's for your safety."

The inspector waved off the lingering security officers, who then joined the others in searching the house.

"I assume I'm coming with you?"

"Yes, you are."

Jaylend motioned with her head at the book and journal on the floor. "Would you mind bringing those along? If there's any chance I get to read or write again, I'd like to have them."

Inspector Fox scooped up them up and flipped through the book. "Okay."

He took her by the arm and led her out the door, escorting her to the street where a robo-transport landed and its doors lifted open.

Before getting inside the vehicle, Fox flipped through the book again while holding Blossom close to his chest. "I read this many, many years ago."

Crying, she smiled through her tears, feeling the enormity of the loss of her house, her books and her writing. "I hope you get to read it again," she said.

Jaylend realized she didn't have the strength to make the tiny step up to get inside the transport. She thought she could face this moment, possibly even with a bit of derring-do, but now her legs refused to move.

"I don't think I can get up." She staggered back a step, and Fox steadied her.

He pressed a button inside the transport and a platform extended out from below the transport. She could step onto the platform and it lifted her inside.

"Oh my God," she sighed as she sat down.

Her world was ending, and she was the only one, it seemed, who cared. Devoid of family for all these years, she'd somehow thought of her students as family, maybe not like her children, but like nieces and nephews.

Anyway, not even the neighbors dared come out to watch. They were all huddled in their homes, unable to do anything to help her.

Those neighbors supported her a thousand times before, and she was grateful. Her only regret was not being able to thank them.

Fox waved his fingers above the console and the door closed.

Jaylend couldn't keep from crying. "Why are you doing this?" she sobbed.

Fox shook his head but said nothing.

"I couldn't get away," she whispered. "This is my home."

Fox released the binds on her wrist and handed her Blossom. "I'm sorry."

As the robo-transport lifted off, Jaylend noticed a group of men with weapons emerge from the homes across the street from her own.

One of the security transports parked on the street exploded, then the other. The men across the street had fired some kind of rocket at them.

"What the—" Fox said and snapped his fingers at the console. They hovered a hundred feet in the air as a plume of black smoke rose past them.

The security officers ran around the yard firing their weapons, but the men with the rocket launcher had slipped away.

Fox seemed to regain his composure and got their robo-van moving. They had moved one street over, and there was a young man in the front yard of the house across the street. He spun something held in his hand at high speed, then released it, and Jaylend noticed a small object rise toward the robo-van. The young man had used a sling, one of the oldest weapons in the book.

There was a soft thud as the object hit the side of the robo-van, then a flash of light, and they descended.

Fox turned away from his computer and waved his hands at the console. "Oh shit," he said, his voice excited and much louder than normal. "Electromagnetic pulse."

The ground rushed up at them and they landed hard, blowing out windows and rupturing the door.

Four men, dressed in the casual garb of Old Town, reached into the open door and pulled Fox and Jaylend out of the robo-van. Three of the men dragged Fox towards the house, and the other helped Jaylend to her feet.

"Can you walk?"

"Yes," Jaylend said, breathless and confused by what had just happened. She realized the man was Tom, whom she'd seen so many times at Decker's Cafe. "I thought I was going to die," she said.

"Not yet," the man said.

He led her towards the house and then into the yard behind it. They emerged one more street over, where Fox, limp and unconscious, was lifted into the back of an electric delivery van.

A quick burst of gun fire erupted from the other street, then an enormous explosion.

"What's happening?"

"We're with The Collective," Tom said. "Do you want to get away from here?"

"Yes, of course."

"Then here we go."

He helped her up into the van and joined her in back.

"Where are we going?"

"Far, far away from here," the man said.

When the door shut, a small light turned on inside the van. "This was not how I thought my day would turn out," she said.

"So far, so good," Tom said.

The van dallied for a while, and Tom seemed tense as they made several turns. Jaylend also stayed tense and realized her hands were shaking even as she gripped Blossom.

"You want some Steady?" Tom asked.

Jaylend shook her head. "I'm sure it's just the adrenaline wearing off."

He pulled a flask from a back pocket and offered it to her. "Brandy?"

Jaylend accepted it and downed a shot. "Thank you."

"What're you reading?"

Jaylend glanced at her lap and realized she had somehow grabbed the journal and the book in the chaos after the crash landing. "Don Quixote."

"Nice," Tom said. "Some days I feel like Don, other days I feel like Pancho."

Jaylend nodded. Then she took another drink of the brandy.

# # # #

Abel found their rendezvous point, a residential street

corner two blocks away from the cafe. There was a bench near the corner with a faded advertisement painted on the back rest. He leaned his back on what used to be a phone number. Up close, he could make out the lines of a face.

It was early evening, but the sun was already setting. He had thought little about it, but it was September and the days were getting shorter. In the cafe's direction, the sky was orange with streaks of red. Overhead, the blue sky darkened to purple.

Someone nearby was cooking, and the smell of garlic and beans and rice made his mouth water. Oh how he wished things could have been simpler. Only two months ago, his mother, defying convention, would have cooked a meal for their family. It was their habit to eat together and talk, and it surprised Abel when his friends were baffled by this practice. They wondered why Abel's family just didn't watch something projected on the wall.

A man carrying a bag loaded with something heavy walked by and glanced at Abel. The man stopped and turned back.

"You know the bus doesn't come around here anymore, right?" the man asked.

"I'm waiting for a friend."

"Would you like a cucumber?"

"Is that a joke?"

The man lifted a cucumber from the bag and held it out. "I have more than I can eat, so I'm taking these to a friend."

"Thank you."

"I rinsed them off so you can just eat it."

Abel bit off the end. It was firm and succulent and tasted of summer.

Before he could thank the man, two security sirens, faint and far away, distracted his attention.

"Good night," the man said and hurried away.

Abel looked in that direction and saw Leah approaching. At her side was Ilasha.

Abel hurried toward them. He couldn't believe it was happening and wanted to cry out in joy.

But as they drew closer, he realized Ilasha was crying, and Leah seemed distraught.

"Hey," he said. "You made it. Ilasha!"

Ilasha stopped crying and smiled, pulling away from Leah to leap into Abel's arms.

"I'm so sorry," Leah said. "I'm so sorry."

"For what? You made it. I can't believe you did it."

The sirens grew closer, and Abel looked at Leah. He understood the concern on her face.

"We have to go," she said.

Abel didn't understand. Of course they were going to go. They'd all go together. Holding Ilasha like this made everything right; he would not let go again.

"Okay," he said. "Lets go."

Leah took his hand and kissed him, pulling him close and breathing through her nose.

He'd never been kissed before, and wasn't sure what else to do, but he liked it and didn't pull away. He felt calmer.

Ilasha snuggled closer into his shoulder, and he thought this must be fine; a good thing, in fact.

Leah pulled away and took a deep breath. "I'm sorry. I wasn't sure if I'd ever get to do that."

"Well..."

As Abel leaned in to do it again, a security drone flew along the street. It flew past them, a brief whisper quiet enough to miss if you weren't listening. Then it turned back and circled above them.

"I thought I lost it," Leah said. "I'm so sorry."

"Oh shit," Abel said.

"Is there somewhere we can go?"

"My contact was going to meet us on the next block."

"Should we go there?"

"Let's try it."

They walked with Ilasha between them, each holding one of her hands. Abel glanced at Leah, and she glanced back. Then they both looked at Ilasha and smiled at each other.

"Thank you for bringing her," Abel said. "I needed a hug."

The drone's circles expanded as it moved along the street with them. Abel didn't want to say it, but he didn't think this was going to work. He just wanted to go for a walk with his sister and Leah. It was a pleasant moment, and he wished it could go on forever.

A boy emerged from between two houses across the street. He set something in a sling and twirled it at his side as he gazed up at the evening sky. When the drone's circle drew nearer to him, he twirled his sling overhead and faster. Then he released it and ducked back between the houses.

Abel watched the launched object rise above the houses. It flashed orange as it reflected the setting sun's blaze, looking for a moment like a shooting star. It neared the drone and burst into a bright white light.

The drone fell and landed in the front yard of a house, bouncing across the garden planted there. A man ran from behind the house and grabbed the drone, struggling to drag it away.

"What was that?" Leah asked.

"I don't know," Abel said, "but let's keep moving."

The man used his hip as leverage and got the drone off the ground. He took two steps but then dropped it and ran away.

Abel looked back. Two security vehicles pulled onto the street and sped up. The lead vehicle went over the curb and stopped in front of the house where the drone crashed. Four security guards piled out of the vehicle and ran behind the house.

The other vehicle stopped on the street next to them and four more security guards got out.

Abel had picked up Ilasha at some point and held her close. With his other arm, he pulled Leah in close.

Her face turned toward his and they kissed.

CHAPTER THIRTY-EIGHT

They locked Ballard in a room at Human Resources. There was a cot, a small table and chair, and a separate bathroom. At a glance, he counted six cameras. There were more, but the exact count didn't matter.

Stanley had escorted him there to enjoy the moment. He could still be watching, hoping to see some sort of breakdown.

Of course, Ballard deserved whatever happened to him now. He should have tracked Leah, coached her on the risk, and made sure she didn't do anything stupid.

The door opened and a visored security guard stepped inside. He motioned for Ballard to sit on the cot.

A woman dressed in standard-issue R1 uniform came in, staring at the computer in her hands. She looked and seemed surprised, as if just remembering where she was.

"Oh, sorry," she said. "You're Ballard Davidson. I'm Karen, from Human Resources."

"We've met," Ballard said. "Three years ago, at a product launch meeting."

"Oh?"

Ballard nodded. "How's Bob?"

Karen glanced at the guard. "He's fine, I guess, but we divorced."

"I'm sorry to hear that."

"He remarried but then got sent to Family Valley, so it's fine."

"Oh, okay."

"Um, you have a visitor. It's your boss."

"Great. Send her in."

Karen glanced at the guard again, then realized she needed to do it and stepped out into the hall. She peeked her head inside again and said, "I'll just be a minute."

When the door opened again, Viktoria entered, followed by Karen.

"There he is," Karen said.

"Indeed, he is," Viktoria said, and smiled at Ballard.

"Do you need anything?" Karen asked. "Coffee or tea maybe?"

Viktoria turned to Ballard, and he shook his head.

"Just the room."

"Oh?" Karen asked.

Viktoria nodded, and Karen and the guard stepped out.

Viktoria grabbed the chair and set it near the end of the cot. "Sorry about all this."

"Me too. I feel like I let you down."

"You didn't. Sometimes organizations have these moments."

"Indeed, they do."

"I'm hoping we can snatch function from the jaws of dysfunction."

"Sure. How can I help?"

Viktoria closed her eyes for a moment. Ballard recognized this as her practice of choosing the best words for any situation, the awkward pauses be damned.

"There was nothing found on your computers which, I suppose you know, since you were the one that wiped them."

"Is this being recorded?"

"No, it's not."

"Then yes, I did that."

Viktoria nodded. "Mind telling me why?"

"The security boys can make anything seem like a problem."

"Being wiped clean looks guilty."

"It allows you to state, 'Nothing was on the computers.'"

Viktoria closed her eyes, but only for a second. "Will they find anything in the inner office?"

"No."

"That's good."

"I used it to cut out the noise so I could think."

Viktoria smiled. "Me too."

Sensing a bit of sympathy, Ballard asked, "Is my family okay? I've had no contact with them."

"Yes."

"Leah and Ilasha? I didn't see them at the apartment."

"They are safe. Nothing to worry about."

"Thank you."

"I want you to know that I was not told of this beforehand. I would have dealt with Stanley's concerns."

"Have his concerns been borne out?"

"Not that I'm aware of. Your daughter's cursive writing teacher, and her recent travel patterns, were the issue."

"What did he think she was doing?"

"He interpreted them as a threat."

"That's preposterous. She couldn't have been a threat to anyone."

"But the suggestion of an issue can lead to consequences, such as assignment to Family Valley."

Ballard nodded. His throat had tightened up, and he couldn't speak at the moment.

"They found no journals, except the one she had with her. It had blank pages, and a few missing pages. Nothing at issue there."

"Good."

"Here's where I need your help. They had granted Stanley great privilege in this minor operation, based on a theory that Leah was attempting to help Abel and Ilasha leave the city. He suggested Leah was enamored with Abel, and might even attempt to accompany him, and attempt to start a new life in the unincorporated areas."

"Oh God, I hope there's nothing to that."

"I need your total honesty, do you have any reason to think that was the case?"

"I have no reason to think that."

"Good. It turns out he was right, because they took her into protective custody doing that."

Ballard's throat tightened up, and he worried he might vomit or pass out or both.

Viktoria looked around the room. "Since we're not being recorded, I can also tell you that this hasn't been a good day for Stanley, either."

"Why's that?" Ballard asked with great effort.

"He ordered an operation in Old Town, to bring in Jaylend, the teacher."

"Oh?"

"He was working off a theory that she was teaching encryption and recruiting young people to the collective."

"Okay."

"They confronted the teacher, but failed to secure her."

"Oh no."

"It gets worse. The Collective took Jaylend and a security team member from the scene. And there was an exchange of gunfire."

"Oh shit."

"It's plausible that Jaylend was connected to The Collective."

"Unless it was the security team member."

Viktoria nodded. "I hadn't thought of it that way."

"Either way," Ballard said. "Poor Stanley. Great on ideas, lousy on execution."

Viktoria chuckled. "Was he great on ideas?"

"No. I just liked that turn of phrase."

Viktoria stood up, still smiling, and put the chair back at the desk.

It seemed the storm had passed. She hadn't even given him a questioning look the entire visit. "What about Leah?" Ballard said and stood up.

Viktoria backed away and two security officers rushed inside, slamming Ballard down on the cot. One guard held an electric prod an inch from Ballard's face, the other held his baton raised and ready to strike.

"I'm sorry," Viktoria said. "I should have mentioned that you had to remain seated."

Sweat burst out on Ballard's face, and his arms were shaking. "What's going to happen?" he asked in a whisper.

"I haven't decided."

# # # #

Leah trembled beneath the cot in her room, her legs pulled up to her chest, and wrapped in the cover. She had likely destroyed her family and would never see them again.

Or worse, they would all live together in ruin and it will all be her fault. Karas would torment her. Mother would shun her. And Father, worst of all, would try to comfort her.

Her father is the only one who cares, and she had let him down. She hated this world, though, and was trying to live the only life possible in opposition to the horror. He wouldn't see that, of course. He was part of the horror.

It was too terrible not knowing what would happen.

In the time she'd spent locked in the room, the only interruptions had been when a guard stepped in, demanded she utter a word to prove she was alive, and then left again.

The room was bare. There was a cot, a sink, and a toilet.

She had crawled out from under the cot a few times, driven by thirst, and told herself she'd be brave and stay on top of the cot. Within minutes, however, she tormented herself with dread and regret, and crawled back underneath.

A guard entered. Looking under the cot, he took a knee and said, "You have a visitor."

"Okay."

"Can you get out from under there, or do you need help?"

"I can do it."

"You can lie on the cot but stay there during the visit."

Even wearing a visor, Leah could tell she disgusted him. Once she crawled on top of the cot, he knocked on the door.

A few minutes later, a second guard held the door open for a woman. It was her father's boss, Viktoria.

Viktoria stood next to the cot, gripping something in her fist.

"Things are fine," Viktoria said. "I hope you believe me. You've been in here a couple of days and I know it hasn't been easy."

"I'd like to see my family."

Viktoria smiled. "After our conversation, that might be what happens."

"Okay."

"First, I want you to appreciate that you are receiving special treatment. Human Resources and Security take a dim view of violations to the Terms of Service. They get that from me, and they like to impress me. To be clear, has anyone harmed you, other than confinement in this room?"

Leah shook her head.

"Use your words."

"No," Leah said. "No one harmed me."

"Great." Viktoria motioned to one guard, who stepped out of the room for a moment and brought in a chair, setting it behind Viktoria.

"I'm going to ask you a few questions," Viktoria said as she sat and scooted a little closer. "Will you answer them?"

"I guess."

"You guess?" Viktoria leaned forward in her chair. "I've had half a dozen people working on this situation, recalling data from the servers, and piecing together everything going on the past few weeks. It's an intriguing series of events, but I'll need your help to understand it all. I need to know you're ready to answer the questions I ask."

"Okay."

"Okay what?"

"Okay, sir. I mean ma'am."

Viktoria shook her head. "I want to hear you say the words, 'I'm ready to answer a few questions.' And it wouldn't kill you to sit up and look at me."

Leah sat up on the cot. "I'm ready to answer a few

questions."

Viktoria offered the thing she'd placed beneath her thigh. "We'll start with an easy one."

The thing was the device used to obfuscate voice. "We found it on Abel's person. He said he got it from you. Is that true?

Leah nodded.

"Words."

"Yes, I gave it to him." Wrapped her arms around herself and rocked.

"Don't worry," Viktoria said. "He tried to protect you, but we want the truth."

Leah choked back a scream of rage. She had done this to Abel. If only she'd not had this idea...

"Where did you get this device?"

Leah stared. Admitting it was Jaylend would condemn her. She could blame some random street vendor from Old Town, but that person would die, like the man she tried to help pick up his bundle. She could blame her sister...

"The truth," Viktoria said.

"Jaylend."

"The writing teacher?"

Leah wanted to answer, but she couldn't speak. Her muscles seemed frozen, and a part of her mind was aware of this but could do nothing to make herself speak. She wobbled her head in acknowledgment.

"Okay," Viktoria said. "You're quite lucky. The luckiest person in this entire city. Do you realize that?"

Leah shook her head no.

Viktoria smiled. "You're lucky because I like your father and want very much for this whole thing to be over so he can get back to work and you and your family can live like you did before. Wouldn't that be nice?"

Leah nodded.

"I like you, as well. I've been looking forward to the day you opted-in and joined us. We would give you a suitable position, not just because your father has an important job and does great things for us, but because I think you can become anything you want in R1. I see a lot of myself in you. I was a bit of a rebel at your age. I understand what it's like to figure out how things work and decide what you want to do about that. I bet you could even have my job, some day, if you want it."

Leah did not make any move at this.

"That's the furthest thing in the world to you right now, but just file that away. And I won't hold a grudge. I'm rather impressed that you got this far with what you and Abel were planning.

"I promise nothing will happen to Abel if you don't want it to. You can even discuss with him what happens. Do you understand? You can talk to Abel. If he wants to go back to his job, he can go back to his job. Now, do you want to talk to him?"

Leah nodded. She was terrified that they would kill Abel, but it was worse to think that he would die without talking to her again.

"Then you need to tell me where was he going with Ilasha."

"He had arranged a place to live in Old Town."

Viktoria leaned back in her chair. "Thank you for answering."

Leah nodded. She should have said, 'you're welcome,' but felt sick inside. She wanted to say as little as possible.

"I find you interesting, Leah Davidson, clever daughter of one of the smartest and most loyal employees I've ever known. I'll keep my promise to you about Abel and your family. Do you believe me?"

Leah looked into Viktoria's eyes and thought about it. Not knowing for sure, she shrugged.

Viktoria laughed. "That's good. Also, I'm proud of you."

CHAPTER THIRTY-NINE

Jaylend wasn't sure where they were, or how long they'd been driving. They had switched vehicles six times. Two of the switches had been under cover of darkness, so she was guessing it had been three days.

She had recognized a few landmarks during their travels—one of which from her youth, well before incorporation, on a trip to visit her aunt—and concluded they were heading to the southeastern corner of Old Town, in what had been a bedroom community suburb.

That suburb had been carved out of farmland, as one farmer after another cashed in on their property. Farming was always tough, but as the economics shifted toward corporate farms, and the loans on tractors grew larger than your ability to sell crops, you either sold out or surrendered it all to the bank.

These suburbs had been among the first to empty, even before incorporation, as the township and county governments struggled to provide water and other basic services.

Having been abandoned for so long, this area was only patrolled sporadically.

Their travel pattern was to drive to a place of cover—a warehouse or a garage—and let Fox, their captive, relieve himself once the drugs had worn off enough to allow him to stand. Then it was back to the van, and another un-welcome dose of drugs for the inspector.

An hour into this leg of the journey, Inspector Fox opened his eyes and looked around in a daze.

"Now where are we?" he asked, his voice thick and slurred. He cleared his throat and stared at Jaylend, waiting for an answer.

Blossom hopped off the bench and licked Fox's face.

"Not sure, myself," Jaylend said. She could offer her theory of their location, but she still understood nothing about their new relationship.

He'd been gentle with her during the arrest. Almost sorry he had to do it. Now he was manacled and chained to the wall of the van, drugged and wearing a diaper. He was weak and confused, needing help.

He shifted into a seated position. "What day is it?"

"I think it's been three days, but I'm not sure."

Fox shook his head and lowered himself back to the van floor.

"The free rides end here," Tom said. He had opened the van's rear doors and stood looking at them.

Jaylend worried at the look of concern on Tom's face. "What does that mean?"

"The next part of our journey is on foot."

"How far?"

"It's a very long walk."

Jaylend was tired of being cooped up inside the van. "Fine. I need to move."

He waved her towards the door and helped her step out. Then he closed the van doors again, leaving the semi-conscious Fox restrained.

They were inside the garage of what once was a suburban home. Yard equipment, tools and children's toys lay abandoned along the wall and scattered across the other bay.

They went into the house. The windows and doors were intact, and the only damage within, despite having been abandoned for over twenty years, was a thick layer of dust. There were fresh jugs of water and satchels of food on a part of the kitchen counter, and bags of gear and clothing on the dining room table.

"What about him?" Jaylend asked, pointing back at the door to the garage.

Tom stopped rummaging through one of the duffel bags and took a deep breath. "Oh, sorry," he said. "He goes, even if I have to carry him. You can either go along or stay."

"You would leave me here?"

"I'd drug you so you slept for three or four days."

"Then what?"

Tom shrugged. "You could stay here a while, I guess."

"Wait," Jaylend said, and sat herself at the table. The chair creaked and shifted, and she slammed her hands down on the dusty table to steady herself. "Why would you rescue me just to leave me behind in an abandoned house in the middle of nowhere?"

"We weren't rescuing you," Tom said. "We were capturing Stetson Fox."

"You just wanted to take a prisoner?"

Tom smiled. "We have big hopes for him."

"Are you going to trade him for one of your own that's been captured?"

"We're hoping he can help us kill the dragons."

"Dragons? You're serious?"

Tom nodded.

"And he's going to be a dragon killer?"

"Not kill them. Help us find them. Then figure out how to steal their gold. Maybe kill them after that… We'll see."

"That guy in the van knows where dragons live."

"I think so. I used to work with Mr. Fox, way back when."

"He thought he knew you."

"We were both investigators for the Federal Prosecutor out of the San Francisco office."

"Wait, if you know him, why did you drug him."

"Can't be too careful. I never had time to ask him if he wanted to do this."

"This wasn't his plan?" Jaylend shook her head. "I'm just dumbfounded."

Tom set one of the gear bags on a chair and opened it up, checking what they had packed inside. Blossom, who had brought a toy from the garage inside, marched from room to room, inspecting the place.

"You don't mean actual dragons?" Jaylend asked. "Or are you tilting at windmills?"

He laughed as he lifted a machete from the gear bag and removed it from its sheath. "That's a hoot. But I mean the actual dragons who destroyed this world. Fox and I used to chase them down. Caught a couple of them, back in the day."

"Dragons."

"Yes. And now they're hidden away in the mountains, sleeping on their piles of gold, oblivious to the problems of the world."

Jaylend shook her head. "I don't know what else to say."

"Just think about whether you'd like to come along. We can always use another set of hands."

"You don't think I'm too old to kill dragons?"

"If you decide to come along, that proves you're not too old."

"Now I know you're mad."

CHAPTER FORTY

Abel could only think of the stupidity of it all, his being orphaned, confined by Human Resources, released, and confined once again. It seemed to be the same room as before, but he wasn't certain.

He wasn't certain of anything.

Leah could have been an informant, but she sure seemed to have tried to help them escape. Maybe a little of both? There was no way to be certain.

It was all just so stupid.

There was Steady on the desk again, but he still would not take it. If they wanted to lace his food with it, fine, although the idea of starving himself didn't sound so crazy.

Of course there was Ilasha to consider, but that might already be out of his reach.

A security officer entered and held the door open for Karen, the woman from Human Resources. "How are we getting along?" she asked.

This was all he needed to complete the cycle of stupidity.

"Would you just kill me already, or whatever it is you want to do to me?"

"Whoa, hey," she said. "I don't think anyone wants that to happen. What would your parents think?"

"You sent them to the herd, remember?"

"Oh. Sorry." Then Karen said, "We prefer to call it Family Valley."

Abel sat on the cot and stared at the floor.

"Well anyway, you have a visitor. A pretty important one, so no sudden movements, okay?"

Abel shrugged. "Sure thing."

The door opened again, and another guard entered, along with a woman. There was a moment of confusion as Karen tried to get out of their way.

Abel wondered how these buffoons outwitted his father and mother, who were clever in all things.

One guard stood next to the cot. He brandished an electric prod and a baton, and motioned for Abel to back up against the wall.

"Do you know who I am?" Viktoria asked.

Abel glanced at her. He'd met her more than once at church performances, but never spoke to her beyond a polite greeting. "You were my father's boss."

Viktoria stepped closer, but stayed well-behind the guard next to the cot. "You have a lot of potential, and I'd like to ask you about your interests. Maybe there's something else we can get you to do that won't leave you stuck in Fulfillment the rest of your life."

"Okay."

"Tell me what you like."

Abel couldn't stop the images of violence in his mind, of punching her, and grabbing the electric prod from the guard and using it on her. His breath shortened and there was a ringing in his ears, but he didn't know how to stop these thoughts.

"Are you alright?" Viktoria asked.

A guard stepped forward and reached out, touching Abel on the shoulder.

Abel jerked back, brushing the hand away.

Then he was on the floor, pain shooting throughout his body and unable to move.

The pain stopped a second later, and he blinked. Both guards stood over him. The electric prod was poised to strike again.

"I told you no sudden movements," he heard Karen say.

"It's alright," Viktoria said. "Help him up. Please help him up."

The guards lifted him back onto the cot. Abel tipped over and pulled his legs up close to his chest.

"I'm going to make this real simple," Viktoria said. "I know you've had it rough, and that Leah likes you, and I'm doing this for her. You listening to me?"

Abel nodded.

"Good. Do you want me to find you a job, or do you want me to just put you out of your misery?"

Abel looked at her. His left hand touched the spot where the prod landed, the right side of his chest, just above his stomach, on the ribs.

He thought of Ilasha, how nice it was to hold her. He had heard her voice, smelled her hair, and felt her breath on his neck.

"Well?" Viktoria asked.

"I'd like to be with my sister. And Leah."

Viktoria stared at him, her head frozen. "I'll see what I can do," she said.

# # # #

Leah was asleep in her room when Karen, from Human Resources, woke her up.

"Come on," Karen said. "You don't want to be late for

your meeting."

Leah looked past Karen, expecting to see a guard in the room, but it was just Karen. "What's going on."

"You get to meet with Abel. I think that was one thing you wanted."

"Yes."

"Well, you're a better negotiator than me, I'll tell you that. I haven't had a day off in two years, although I don't know that I would do anything different if I had a day off, not since my husband left me."

Leah sat up. "Let's go."

"Don't you want to shower?" Karen asked. "Get cleaned up or whatever? I brought you a change of clothes."

It had been a few days since last she washed. She hadn't even brushed her teeth. "I suppose. Do you know if Abel has cleaned up and changed clothes?"

Karen shook her head. "I don't think so."

"Then I don't want to either. Let's go."

"Oh alright, little miss bossy."

"I'm sorry, but should I not have said that?"

"Oh no, it's fine. I just never would have said anything like that."

"Sure." Leah stepped past her and opened the door.

"Wait for me," Karen said, laughing.

Leah didn't feel the need to join her in the laugh.

Abel was in the conference room, seated at the head of the table. Two armed guards stood behind him, and two more on either side of the table at its midpoint. Karen pointed to the chair at the other end of the table.

"I'd like to hug him," Leah said.

Karen shook her head. "I was told you need to sit

here."

Abel watched from his place at the table. He was only ten feet away, but it seemed two miles with the guards in the way.

"Hey," Leah said, waving to him. "You okay?"

Abel shrugged. "I've been better."

"Was it better when we kissed?"

Abel smiled. "Yes."

Leah turned back to Karen. "I'd like to speak with Viktoria."

"She's not coming in until after your conversation with Abel is over."

Leah sat down. "I'd like pen and paper."

"What?" Karen looked at the guards, then around the room. "What for?"

"I'd like you to deliver a note to Viktoria for me."

"I'm not sure we have paper."

"I bet you do," Leah said. "I'll speak to Abel while you go look."

After Karen left the conference room, Leah said, "Have they treated you well?"

"Well enough. It is Human Resources, after all. They work for the corporation, not us."

Karen returned with two sheets of paper and a pen. "People thought I was crazy, asking for this."

"Tell those people they are the crazy ones," Leah said.

She tested the pen in the lower corner of the top sheet of paper. It was blue ink. Its flow was far from smooth, but it'd be good enough for what she needed.

Leah jotted the note using cursive and didn't bother signing her name.

She folded the paper once and handed it to Karen. "I'm sure Viktoria would prefer you don't look at it. Just deliver it."

Karen scoffed. "Well, listen to little miss bossy pants."

Leah held Karen's gaze. She learned from her father that a calm demeanor often convinces the unsure to do your bidding. You just have to remain silent until they speak again.

"Okay, well, I guess I'll go deliver this." Karen left the conference room.

"Are you okay?" Abel asked.

Leah shook her head at him. "Of course not," she said. "I'm here."

Abel smiled.

"Have you heard anything about Ilasha?"

"No. Have you?"

"No."

"I'm worried."

"Me too."

They sat and stared at each other. Soon their breathing was synchronized, and it was difficult to keep from getting up to hug him, or at least touch his hand.

Viktoria entered the conference room, followed by Karen.

"You're ready?" Viktoria asked.

Leah nodded.

"Ready for what?" Karen asked. "I have no idea what's happening."

Viktoria snapped her fingers at the guards and swirled her hand, the same motion, Leah noted, used with computers to send an app away. The guards left the room.

"Wait, where are they going?" Karen asked.

"You too," Viktoria said. "I'd like the room."

"Is that a good idea?"

Viktoria nodded.

After Karen left and closed the door, Viktoria asked, "How did you know I read cursive?"

"Just a guess. Either way, I thought I'd get your attention."

"Well, say what you'd like to say to him."

Leah closed her eyes. "If you don't mind, I'd like to be alone with him."

"For how long?"

"Five minutes?"

"Three."

"Okay."

Viktoria laughed. She glanced at Abel and then stepped out, closing the door behind her.

Leah and Abel got up and rushed towards each other. They embraced. Leah moved her face toward Abel's and they kissed.

"What did you do?" Abel asked, his voice just a whisper.

"I'm opting in," Leah murmured. "I thought I would die before I ever did that, but now I know I have to do it."

"Wait. Why do you have to do it?"

"Because I love you."

"But we're just sixteen."

"I won't marry," Leah said. "Not yet."

"You think they'll let us see each other?"

Leah pulled away to look him in the eye. "No."

"No?"

"I made a deal they'd send you somewhere to live with Ilasha, but I don't think she'll honor it. Once I opt in, she can do whatever she wants."

"Then I'll kill myself."

"No. Ilasha needs you, and I think she'll keep you with her. She needs you to take good care of her. I need you to stay alive until I can get back to you."

She kissed him and felt his tension drain away. They rested their heads on each other.

"I love you too," Abel said.

"So you'll marry me?"

"Yes. Someday."

"Good."

There was a knock on the door and then Karen leaned her head inside. "Everything okay in here? You were whispering so quietly the microphones couldn't pick it up."

She placed a computer on the table and pointed at Leah. "I was told you're going to opt-in?"

Leah sat at the table and scrolled through the agreement. "I don't see the clause about Abel and Ilasha living together."

"I don't know what you're talking about."

"Please call Viktoria and ask her about it."

"You're going to get me in big trouble here, little miss bossy pants."

Leah looked at Karen, keeping her face calm, intent on waiting.

"Hang on," Karen said and stepped out of the room.

"Do you know what you're doing?" Abel whispered.

"No. Just asking for what I want."

Karen stepped back inside. "You must be something special, there, little missy."

Karen waved her hand above the computer and the screen updated.

Leah read the document again and, this time, she saw the clause specifying that Abel and Ilasha would live together.

"Okay," Leah said. "I'm ready."

Karen made another hand wave above the computer screen and a box appeared for Leah's hand prints. As she pressed first one hand, and then the other, she leaned forward so that they could scan her retinas at the same time.

Then Karen did the same to act as the first witness.

"Abel?" Karen asked. "I need you to witness, as well."

A few seconds later, the transaction was complete, and Leah had opted in to the Terms of Service for the corporation known as R1.

CHAPTER FORTY-ONE

Jaylend, Tom and Stetson Fox were on the fifth day of their escape on foot. The hike was supposed to have taken three days, but now it seemed they were lost.

At least Jaylend thought they were lost. Tom did not because the stations along the path to camp were not in fixed locations. There was no map.

"We're never lost," Tom said, "because the place we're going is never in just one place. It's mobile, this place, and I'm just solving the puzzle to catch it before it moves again."

"Remind me about the shifting locations," Fox said. He had asked little of Tom during the journey once he understood what had happened. Instead, he'd been talking with Jaylend about Cervantes and Shakespeare and Leonard.

Jaylend wanted to hear the answer to Fox's question, as well. Their journey seemed impossible, more impossible than surviving in Old Town with R1 intent on destroying them.

Tom had explained that the impossibility of it is what makes it possible. "The obstacle is the way," he had said, quoting Marcus Aurelius. "If they think it's easy, or even just possible, they'll defend against it."

"I still don't understand why you both believe in dragons," Jaylend said. "You must have been wearing a visor for too long."

Fox stopped and studied her. Despite five days of hiking, the lack of food, and the terrible sleep, he looked vibrant and alive. The times she'd met him before, back when he was an investigator, he'd looked older, tired, almost listless. Now he seemed about to laugh.

"You who is such a fan of Don Quixote, you don't know about dragons?"

"Dragons were visions, the conjuring of a man suffering dementia, and who also had read too many books about chivalry and dragons. What's your excuse?"

"They're a metaphor used to describe the billionaires from before incorporation."

"I don't understand," Jaylend said.

"Keep walking, please," Tom said. "Stetson will explain, but you both must follow." He had gotten ahead of them by several dozen feet and had picked up speed.

Jaylend, carrying Blossom in her arms, a heavy pack on her back, and with canteens of water hanging from her belt and slapping against her hips, was more tired now than she had ever remembered feeling before in her life. "Do you think he'll get us there, or are we just following a mad man into the wilderness?"

"I hope he gets us there."

"Great. So tell me about the dragons and billionaires."

"Before the collapse of America, as the economy faltered, and disease swept through the population, and the climate crisis turned into a disaster, the billionaires were preparing for the worse."

"The bunkers. I remember."

"Even when the great climate migration started, they had already built sanctuaries for themselves, hidden away in remote valleys, shielded by mountains, in places no one could ever find them."

"They were like castles, right? But underground."

Fox laughed. "They were entire cities, with power plants, water works, and food stores stocked for decades. At the center, enclosed in a climate controlled fortress, was the dragon's lair for him and his wife, or lovers, or both."

"That sounds impossible."

"A few of them would chip in, and so they commanded enough wealth to do anything they wanted. The government, what remained of the government, was so overwhelmed with problems, they did nothing. Even if they cared about it, they couldn't devote anything to dealing with it. Politicians had curried favor with the billionaires all along, accepting their money, doing them favors, and planning to join them in the bunker."

"They all did this?" Jaylend asked. "Even Ophrah?"

"I'm not sure about her, but there were thousands of billionaires. Even as the economy was collapsing, they manipulated stocks to the end, and siphoned off wealth for themselves. Convinced things would not get better, and that they may not be safe from the hordes of desperate people, they created hundreds of remote sanctuaries."

"How could they get away with it?"

Stetson took Blossom in his arms. "A city in the mountain needs tens of thousands of people to function. Those at the top invited friends and family, who in turn invited others, and so on, until all the slots were filled. The disaster was so bad that people were grateful for a chance to live in sanctuary."

"And you know where these sanctuaries are?"

"I have a few guesses."

"Just a few?"

"It was quite the clique at the top, so we assumed they

were all in contact with each other, sharing tips on how to keep their support staff happy and fertile. The last time I looked into it, they had gone tribal, exchanging daughters to enrich the gene pool, and sharing labor and ideas to keep their cities functioning."

Jaylend stopped to calm herself, wanting to scream at the stupidity of it all. "And R1 didn't want to stop them?"

Fox chuckled. "Hell, R1 is nothing but a dragon's lair hiding in plain sight. If the executives put in excellent work, and avoid being sent to Family Valley, they go to Heaven for their retirement."

Killing a dragon sounded like a good idea. "I want to go with you."

Fox laughed. "Let's see if we can inspire Tom to find our first camp."

Tom, farther ahead than before, stood on the crest of a hill, shading his eyes.

"The thing that bothered me," Fox said, "was that the billionaires could have done something. They could have eased the suffering, fixed the infrastructure, and rebuilt the economy."

"I had been hoping the government might do some of that."

Fox laughed, catching his breath. "Government serves at the pleasure of the wealthy."

"So now they're like city-states," Jaylend said.

"The image of dragons sleeping on piles of gold resonates better."

When they caught up to Tom, he was still on the crest of the hill. Below them, in a clearing of trees, was a series of three tents, camouflaged.

Two men and two women stood outside the tents looking up at them, waving.

Tom waved back. "I told you I'd find it."

CHAPTER FORTY-TWO

Her father met Leah in the lobby of the Human Resources building. "Where's Mom and Karas?" she asked.

"At the apartment," he said as he hugged her.

"Are they okay?"

"They were treated rather well. Ready to go?"

Leah hesitated, looking around the lobby. The benches along the wall were empty. The secure inner entrance, guarded by four armed security officers, was quiet. The service counter windows were empty except for a single clerk, her face obscured by the visor.

"What about Abel and Ilasha?"

Her father shook his head, seeming impatient to get going. "I don't know, Princess. I was told about your release, but nothing else."

"Can you ask?"

"I'll do what I can to find out."

They rode the train, having to change at the downtown station. Tired of the long ride, and hungry after the ordeal, she asked, "Why didn't you call a robo-van? Are you in trouble?"

"It's not an option for me."

"Are you mad?"

He shook his head and offered a quick smile.

Leah didn't ask anymore questions, but she wanted to scream. If she'd caused them trouble, why didn't he just say so?

At the apartment, her mother was in the front room watching a projection.

"Hey," Leah said.

Her mother offered a quick smile and returned to the projection.

"Okay," Leah said as she went to her room.

She stopped in the doorway. They'd taken away all of her things. The sketches and artwork, once pinned to the wall, were missing. A small table replaced her desk. On top of it was a new computer, like the one her sister had. They also replaced her bed with a larger one and plain bedding.

The room felt different and for a moment she wondered if she'd somehow gone into the wrong one. The walls had been painted, and the floor replaced. Inside the closet, all her clothing was gone. In its place were seven identical R1-uniforms, like those her sister wore, but plain, with no adornment or customization.

"Mom?" she called. "Can you come here, Mom?"

But her mother didn't come, and Leah walked out to the front room. "Mom," she said. "Didn't you hear me?"

"I'm busy, Leah," she said. "Whatever it is, can we talk about it later? Or talk to your father about it."

Leah knocked on her father's bedroom, but he wasn't there. She heard Karas talking inside her room and went in, thinking she'd find him. Karas was alone and reclining on her bed, her pocket computer propped on her chest.

"Don't you knock?"

"Sorry, I was looking for Dad. He's not in his room."

"He's not here, either, idiot."

Leah took a breath. Her sister was always mean, but this was cruel. "Do you know where he is?"

"In his inner office."

Leah knocked on that door, but again there was no response. He locked the door, as always, so she couldn't check herself. "Dad," said. "Can I talk to you?"

"He's busy," her mother called from the front room. "Can you please just wait? I'm watching something."

Leah returned to Karas's room, this time knocking on her way inside. "Can I talk to you?"

"No," Karas said, lowering her pocket computer. "I'm talking with Ashton, so beat it."

"Why is Mom being such a bitch to me?"

"You mean other than the bullshit stunt you pulled that got Ilasha taken away from us and almost got us all killed. Is that what you mean?"

"I was doing what I thought was best for Ilasha?"

"No, you were doing what you thought would make Abel fall in love with you."

"Shut the hell up."

"I'm with Mom on this one. I don't want to see you, either, so close the door on your way out."

Karas lifted her pocket computer. "Sorry, Ashton," she said. "I'm back, it was just my little—"

Leah rushed to the bed and knocked the computer from Karas's hands.

"Are you out of your mind?" Karas said. She shoved Leah against the wall.

Leah's mind filled with a scream of rage and she grabbed Karas's throat, digging her nails into the flesh. Karas flailed back at her, slapping Leah's arms and face, screaming until she stopped breathing.

Karas fell back onto the bed, pulling Leah's hair.

"Stop it!" her father yelled. He pulled Leah off of

Karas, and wrapped her in his arms, dragging her out of the room.

He took her into her room and set her down on the bed. "You'll stay here?"

She nodded.

"I'm going to check on Karas. Don't move."

"I'll stay."

Leah heard her sister crying, so at least she hadn't killed her, but she also didn't understand where that rage had come from. She had wanted to hurt her sister before but had never imagined something like this.

Leah lay back on her bed and stared at the ceiling. She tried to focus on her breathing, but thoughts forced their way into her mind. Would she ever get to write her thoughts in a journal, again? Where was Ilasha? Now that she had opted-in, when would she be assigned a job? Would she see Jaylend, or Abel, ever again?

"That's it?" her mother said. She stood in the doorway, staring, nothing revealed by her face. "You do everything you can to destroy this family, and now you just lie there like nothing happened."

"Mom, I'm sorry. I don't know what came over me."

"If there is so much as a bruise on my daughter, I'm calling security." She turned and left.

"Mom," Leah called after her. "I'm your daughter too."

A few minutes later, Karas came in. She lingered in the doorway, holding a hand to her throat.

"I'm very sorry, Karas," Leah said. "Please forgive me —"

"Just shut up," Karas said. "You've had your fun. I'm sick of you, and I'll be glad to see you go."

"What are you talking about?"

"They're discussing it right now. Mom wants you out of here."

"Leave me alone."

"Maybe you can go live with Ilasha. She's as much your sister as I am, you know."

"What?"

"You and I have the same father, and you and Ilasha have the same mother. Tyra birthed you and everything, but it wasn't her egg."

"What are you talking about?"

"Ashton told me, and now it makes sense. It was Viktoria's egg and Dad's sperm. Mom was just the surrogate."

"That's insane."

"Not at all. It's an official program and everything. When I was a fetus, I had gene editing to make me perfect. They had to make a deal to get me, which is why Mom had to birth you. You're just my half-sister."

"I don't believe you."

"It's true, you can ask Dad. I'm perfect, but you're a princess. You're one of the boss's special babies."

Leah shook her head. Her sister had said cruel things before, but this was crazy talk.

"Yeah," Karas said. "You and about a thousand other babies, all half-sisters, born of the boss's harvested eggs, fertilized by random men from R1, and birthed by their wives."

"That explains why Mom hates me."

"Yeah, well, I just want you to know why Mom is sending you away. No hard feelings or anything."

Leah glanced at Karas. "If it's a choice between you and me, the corporation will pick me."

# # # #

Leah's father called her into his inner office. When the door was secure, and she sat on the sofa, he said, "Karas told you about your genetic mother?"

Leah nodded.

"You're still our daughter. We love you as much as we love Karas."

"Does Mom know you're saying that?"

"She loves you, Leah. She had quite a scare these past few weeks. I never should have agreed to bringing Ilasha in here. It was too much."

"Is everything Karas said true?"

"What else did she say?"

"That Mom wants me out of here."

He didn't answer. Instead, he sat next to her on the couch. "She said that, but it's not what she wants now."

"And what do you want?"

"I want us to be a family."

Leah pulled her legs up and hugged them, tipping over on the sofa. "When I heard those rumors about hundreds of the girls in the city being Viktoria's, it didn't occur to me I was one of them." Leah looked around the room, felt the walls closing in, and wanted to crawl under something, like she did in the cell at Human Resources. "I don't know what to do."

"Well, you're going to stay here with us. Okay?"

Leah looked at him. She wasn't sure he was her father. Something about him looked different, foreign. He was a close copy of her father, but it wasn't her father.

"What about Abel?" she asked. "Did she do what she promised?"

"No."

She sat up. "Oh God. What? What did she not do?"

"Abel and Ilasha get to live together..."

"Okay."

"She sent them to Family Valley."

"To live with their parents?"

He shook his head. "Abel is to work as a wrangler."

"What the hell is a wrangler?"

"He'll help manage the herd."

"The herd of humans?"

He nodded his head, lowering his eyes.

"I'd still like to go live with him, if that's okay with you."

He looked at her and she realized he was crying. "You don't want to live with us?"

"I don't think Mom or Karas want me here."

"I know it's tough right now, but please let's try for a little while."

Tears filled her eyes, and her throat tightened. "I love you, Dad, but I also feel that I hurt Abel and Ilasha, and I'd like to help them if I can."

He took a moment to catch his breath. "I don't think Human Resources, Security, or my boss will allow that. At least not right away."

"What are you saying?"

"If you take a position with R1, and show you can follow the rules, and fit in, then you might have that option later on."

"How much longer is later on?"

He seemed reluctant and pursed his lips. "A couple years. Maybe three."

"Three years?"

"You are just sixteen. You have a lot of life ahead of you."

"This is so unfair."

"I know it's not what you wanted to hear," he said, "but we're very fortunate. This whole thing started because Abel and Ilasha's parents tried to escape the city. That's why they were sent away."

The light above the door blinked, meaning they

needed him in the apartment.

"I better see what's going on," he said. "You going to stay here?"

Leah nodded. "I'll be out in a little while."

Leah stared at the plain, white ceiling for several minutes, trying to focus on her breathing, but seeing images of Abel and Ilasha in her mind. She could feel Ilasha's hand in her own as they hurried along the sidewalk, trying to get away.

Leah saw Abel's brown eyes staring into her own, unblinking, true, and lovely. She smelled his breath when they held other. She still tasted his lips on her own.

When at last she found him again, would those things still be the same for her? And would her heart pound as it did each time he was near?

She left the inner office and wandered around the apartment. Her father was speaking to someone via computer in his room. Karas was also talking on her computer to Ashton. They spoke in whispers, laughed, and returned to whispers again.

In the front room, her mother sat on the sofa, a visor on her head, oblivious to everything but the images projected before her face.

Leah left the apartment and walked up the stairs to the roof.

The sun was setting beyond the hills, and a warm breeze brought smells of oil, smoke and dust.

She walked to the edge of the roof. In the buildings all around them, synchronized light flickered in all the windows as every apartment was projecting the same story on the wall.

Below her, on the street, people walked along, their

visors pulled down before their face.

Everyone everywhere in the entire city was unaware that she stood there on the roof at that moment. The surveillance A.I. might know it, but it wouldn't alert anyone for quite a while.

If she fell to the cement below, still no one would notice for quite some time.

She turned to the south. There, a hundred miles away, Abel was doing something, maybe starting his life as a wrangler, or maybe just helping Ilasha get ready for bed.

Abel might wonder at this very moment what she was up to here in the city.

She decided that moment to do whatever it would take to see him again. She would follow the rules if she had to, or break them if need be, but no one would stop her from seeing him again unless they killed her.

"Good night Abel," she said to the southern view. "I'll see you soon."

ABOUT THE AUTHOR

Mickey Hadick lives near Lansing, Michigan where he has worked on short stories, novels, screenplays, and books for the past couple of decades.

Whenever possible, he's telling stories, telling jokes, or messing around with computers.

He lives with his wife, two cats, and as many dogs as possible. He also chases after his adult children as needed.

If you enjoyed this story and would like to know when the next book in this series is available, join him at:

MickeyHadick.com

ACKNOWLEDGMENTS

276

Many thanks to my wife, Mary and my now-adult children who have lived with my writing efforts for many years now.

Thanks and gratitude to Shelly Willoughby who provided feedback and helped shape the story.

PARKSIDE BOOKS

Be sure to check out the other titles available at:

ParksideBooks.net

Make sure you get in on deals and keep up with Mickey by signing up to receive the Mickey Picayune at:

MickeyHadick.com/joinus/

ERRORS

Although Parkside Books goes to great lengths to fix all errors before we go to print, we're not perfect. If you see a problem, please notify us via email at:

support@parksidebooks.net

MICKEY HADICK